HOLIDAY INTRUSION

A DARK & KNOTTY CHRISTMAS TALE

NORA ASH

To you, who's working customer service this holiday season.
This too shall pass.

TRIGGER WARNING

This dark romance contains dark subject matters that may be triggering for some.

Please visit www.nora-ash.com for a list of specific themes

ABOUT THE AUTHOR

Nora Ash writes thrilling romance and sexy paranormal fantasy.

Visit her website to learn more about her upcoming books.

WWW.NORA-ASH.COM

ONE

'TIS THE SEASON

"Someone needs to run you over with an eighteen-wheeler, you useless bitch."

"And a merry Christmas to y—" is all I manage in return, before the call disconnects.

"Quick! It's twenty-three seconds past eight!"

I jerk my head to the side just in time to see Dana rip her headset off and toss it on her desk with all the triumph of a victorious Olympian. "Fuck, the Horrible Hordes of Holiday Hell are getting ragier by the day."

"I can't wait for my Christmas Eve shift. If you think this is bad, imagine the joy of telling parent after parent that their kid's present won't show up in time just *hours* before they're supposed to be opening them."

I quickly click the button to log off and wince at the flashing box on my screen indicating that there were still fifteen people waiting to yell at a customer service representative. Someone's going to be dealing with some angry emails in the morning.

"I swear, after working here, I understand why suicide rates boom in December." Dana gives me a dramatic eyeroll. "No wonder they have to pay us extra this month. Anyway, let's *go*. Michael texted that he'll have wine and a hot bath ready, and if I get home fast, I might stay awake long enough to give him a thank-you bang this time. Poor guy's not gotten laid since the third."

I wave a hand in dismissal. "Go. Take care of your guy's blue balls. I've gotta fill out an incident report first."

Dana grimaces. "Shit, another one?"

"Well, that depends—does suggesting that I need to get run over with a eighteen-wheeler count as a death threat?" I arch my eyebrows in mock interest. I'm pretty sure my latest angry customer isn't going to rock up to McCain Enterprises in a truck, intent on hunting down the unfortunate customer rep who had to tell him his daughter won't be getting a dollhouse after all. If for no other reason than parking that thing Downtown Mattenburg ten days before Christmas would be a nightmare.

However, McCain Enterprises *"takes all threats to their valued employees very seriously,"* and if I don't fill out a report and the jerk lodges a formal complaint—and *boy,* did he sound like the type who's going to lodge a formal complaint—my manager will listen to his call and promptly give me a written warning for not filing a report. Something-something insurance liability.

"Ouch. Where would he even park that thing?" Dana gives me a comforting smile. "Well, guess I'll see you tomorrow for another round of Holiday Hell."

"Can't wait. Have a good night."

She grins. "It'll be better than yours."

It absolutely will. My job as a customer service rep for McCain Enterprises' online toy store has improved significantly since Dana started in August, but I'm painfully aware that once we go home for the night, she has a full life with a husband who adores her.

I don't even have a cat.

My other colleagues empty out about as fast as Dana, giving me sympathetic waves as they pass my desk.

I wouldn't mind having to fill out these stupid things, if each one didn't take half a goddamn hour to complete.

WHEN I'M FINALLY DONE, the entire floor is Ghost City.

I turn off my computer and grab my bag in ten seconds flat, then rush for the door. I don't live in Mattenburg proper, but in a larger suburb some thirty minutes out by train. Connections are great until around a quarter to nine—then they drop to once every ninety minutes. *No thank you to stumbling home in the freezing cold at freaking midnight!*

I'm almost halfway down the hall to the main elevators when the overhead lights flicker, then die.

"Shit," I mutter, stumbling to a halt when I'm plunged into unexpected darkness. My night vision is terrible at the best of times, and the corridor is windowless.

I fumble for the wall, determined not to miss my train, but the second my fingertips skim over its surface, the lights flick back on. Happy days!

I rush to the last few yards and press the elevator button.

Nothing happens.

I frown and press the button again. The usual blue light doesn't flash at my touch, and the display above showing which floor the elevator is on is also dead. No mechanical sounds emit from the elevator shaft, either.

"*Shit.*" I can take the stairs, but we're on the tenth floor. If I do that, I'm absolutely missing my train.

Or...

Or I can take the executives' elevator. Us mere drones aren't allowed in there, but it's so late, no one will even know.

I turn around and sprint around the corner, then down the short hallway hosting the few managerial offices on this floor. Most higher-ups don't spend significant time with lowly customer service agents. Truth be told, I'm pretty sure the only reason we're as high up as the tenth floor is that by the time the first-floor office where the other half of the team works outgrew their space, this was the only available office in the building.

When I hit the button for the executives' elevator, it flashes blue with a merry bing, and a soft whirring from behind the doors makes me sigh with relief. If I run all the way from McCain Tower to Central, I'll make my train.

When the doors open, I do a double-take. The interior is lined with polished mahogany and brass accents, and each wall is clad in gilded mirrors. Apparently the fancy people running the place can't possibly travel in anything but luxury—not even between floors.

I step into the small car having never felt more like a Medieval peasant. Someone's even decorated it for the holidays with a lush branch of mistletoe dangling from the ceiling. Meanwhile, a few days ago, my office manager tore one of the newbies a new one for daring to decorate his monitor with a bit of tinsel.

Apparently, holiday cheer is reserved for our betters.

Quietly seething, I hit the button for the ground floor. I'm not paid to get in the festive spirit, but it was easier to swallow when I thought the Grinch-like approach to Christmas was a company-wide policy.

I'm barely done glaring at the mistletoe when the elevator slows to a stop and the doors roll open with another merry tune. At the ninth floor.

Oh, shit. I have a moment's worth of panic at the realization that I'm about to get busted for riding the executives' elevator, but the enormous, suit-clad man who steps through doesn't even glance at me. His focus is glued to the stapled stack of papers in his hands. Ninth floor is accounting, so I'm guessing he's absorbed by what's likely to be the staggering projections for our Christmas revenue.

He hits the button for the ground floor without so much as acknowledging my presence, even though I have to squeeze up against the wall to ensure no parts of us touch. It's not a tiny elevator, but it's not huge either, and this man takes up *a lot* of space.

I sneak a closer look at my ride-buddy. Only alphas get that big, and *yup*—his wide-set shoulders and square jaw confirm my suspicions. Even his fancy suit can't fully hide the thick muscles cording his biceps.

It's not surprising, I guess. We rarely see any alphas on my floor, but a lot of the executive positions are filled by them. Bossy jerks like the power, though I am surprised to see one in accounting—they tend to be more about barking orders and taking charge of mergers than fiddling with numbers.

He does seem oddly familiar, though. He looks young —only a faint salt-and-pepper touch to his dark hair suggests he might be a bit older than first glance would suggest. Thirties, perhaps? There's a bit of scruff on his cheeks—he probably shaved this morning, but alpha testosterone is no joke.

And this guy's definitely loaded with it. I can sense it in the air, his alpha musk, even though my nose only picks up on his expensive cologne. It's making my heart thud behind my ribs, an awareness washing over me that I can only liken to being in the presence of a hopefully-docile predator. My entire body is alert and hyper-focused on the giant male trapped in the confined space with me.

Who the heck is this guy?

I narrow my eyes as I study him. High cheekbones, soft lips with a haughty tilt, and—oh *shit*, no!

I suck in a sharp breath before I can stop myself.

Adam McCain finally looks up from his report and glances at me, alerted by my gasp.

Yeah. Adam McCain—as in the CEO of McCain Enterprises. On the list of Forbes' 500 most powerful business moguls. And known around my office as a grade-A prick.

I've never had the displeasure of meeting him in person before—I've only seen him in passing twice during my past four years working here—but my last manager had the misfortune to be called into a meeting with him right before she cleared her desk and left a shaking, snotty mess, never to be seen again. No one knows what the hell happened to make the almighty CEO obliterate a lowly office manager like that, but through October, we all had a betting pool centered around who could tell the most terrifying Halloween story featuring McCain as the Bogeyman.

An especially vivid retelling of a sexy psycho killer flashes before my mind's eye when McCain frowns at me and says, "You're not an executive."

It's a very simple statement, but said in his deep, rumbling alpha bass, and with his intense, dark stare focused entirely on me, it makes an unholy mix of shame and fear claw its way up my spine.

"I, uh... No?" The words squeak out of me like a question. "I'm—I'm sorry, the other elevator wasn't working, and I need to catch my train."

He opens his mouth, undoubtedly to tell me I'm fired and he'll be billing me to have the elevator professionally cleaned of my peasant germs, but before he can eviscerate me, the elevator gives an odd sort of *lurch*—and then the lights flicker out.

I don't have claustrophobia, and I'm not afraid of the dark. Not separately, at least.

However, combine an enclosed space with pitch blackness? Turns out I definitely have a phobia of *that*.

"Oh my God! *Oh my God!*" I'm not even aware of the high-pitched nature of my squeals. All I sense is that I'm *trapped*, and I can't *see*. I flail for purchase and smack something solid that promptly goes flying and hits the floor with a *thunk*.

"*Fuck*," McCain grumbles, then huffs a breath when my scrambling hands reach his shirt sleeves, and I yank on them in mindless search for safety.

Looking back on it, I'd never be able to explain why the man, who not two seconds ago nearly made me wet myself with terror, suddenly feels like a safe thing to cling to, but my panicked animal brain doesn't give a single flying fuck.

I don't manage to move the mountain of a man closer to me—instead a ripping sound and a heavy metallic clonking on the floor suggests I've torn his cuffs.

"All right, *calm down*," he rumbles, and some small part of me instantly does calm. However, it only amplifies my need to not be alone in the dark.

Sobbing unintelligibly, I take a step and bump against his body, again grasping at his suit in an attempt to get closer still.

McCain, possibly realizing I'm about to shred his expensive suit in my efforts to climb him like a monkey, quickly wraps an arm around my body and arms, immobilizing me against the bulk of his torso. "Breathe. It's just a power outage. *Calm yourself.*"

Ooh, he's warm.

I breathe in a lungful of his heady cologne, and instantly I begin to relax. *Mm, he smells like... rum-spiced chai and a cozy sweater on a cold winter's day.*

I breathe again, about to bury my nose in his chest and shamelessly sniff him, when he mercifully releases his grip on me and takes a half-step back to fish his phone out of a pocket.

The shock of our separation and the faint light from his phone allows enough of my brain to reactivate that I finally realize what I'm doing.

God, Eve, you absolute psycho!

I jerk back until I hit the wall, suddenly wishing the damn elevator would plummet to the ground and take both of us to our deaths in the process. *Mortified* does not begin to describe what I feel right now. What the *hell* was that? He's a stranger—no, worse than that—he's my boss' boss' boss' boss, and here I am *sniffing* the man? What is *wrong* with me?

"It's McCain. Is the power out everywhere? Right. I'm stuck in the executive elevator, around third floor. I expect to be out in five minutes, tops."

A beat. And then, "I don't care. Make it a priority."

I grimace at the alpha barking orders into his phone—if I'd gotten a say, I'd have voted to be *a lot* nicer to the maintenance team currently holding our fate in their hands, but at least being stuck in here with the CEO should mean a swift rescue. Even if his manners are appalling.

McCain switches off his phone with an annoyed grunt, and the elevator is once again cast in complete darkness.

I draw in a shuddering breath and dig my nails into my palms in an attempt at keeping myself in check. *Do not sniff that man, Eve. Sniffing random alphas will* not *make this situation any better!*

"I've never met a grown woman this afraid of the dark."

I don't even care that he's not so much as trying to keep the disdain from his voice; he's talking, and for some idiotic reason, my brain finds it calming.

"I'm not."

He scoffs. "My report and cufflinks would suggest otherwise."

"I'm fine when it's not in such a confined space hovering God-knows-how-many yards above the ground," I bite.

I can practically hear his eyeroll, but he doesn't say anything else.

The silence is awful. I know he's in there with me; I can still smell him, still hear his slow breathing and sense his huge mass filling up the space, but the quietness makes my all-too trigger happy anxiety rear its head again.

I almost ask him about his Christmas plans at least five times in the long minutes we wait in silence, but despite my fervent wish that he'll speak again and magic away this awful, clawing terror in my gut, I manage to restrain myself.

Eventually, when it's definitely been more than five minutes and I don't think I can take it anymore, I squeak, "How long did they say it'd take?"

"They didn't." He sounds agitated—*way* more agitated than before, and I swallow thickly at the stutter at the base of my spine.

Angry alpha. I don't care how civilized we all are, I dare anyone stuck in a tiny cube with a cranky alpha to not feel at least a sliver of primal unease.

Growling a low curse, he pulls out his phone and hits the redial button.

I hear the muted sound of the phone ringing, but it doesn't connect.

"Fuck!" he snarls, hurling the device to the floor. The distinctive *crunch* of dead electronics plunges us into darkness once more. "Goddammit!"

He *broke* his *phone.*

"Why would you do that?!" I yell before I can stop myself. "Mine's out of battery! How are we gonna get in touch with anyone now?"

"It's your goddamn fault!" he growls, and despite the outrageous accusation, my own temper is thoroughly cowed by his aggression. "You *reek* of fear, and I can't fucking *think*. Just... *come here.*"

I blink at the command, but my body obeys before my brain gets any input on the matter.

This time, he's the one reaching for me. The second I'm close enough, he clamps his strong arms around my body and pulls me in tight.

Instant warmth floods me from where we touch, followed by immediate calm.

McCain groans softly into the darkness above my head. "God, that's better."

"Um...?" I don't quite dare voice the question, partly because this is so far past embarrassing I can't fully process it, and partly because I don't want him to let go. For whatever stupid, primitive reason, turns out I'm *all* about alphas in a crisis. *Mortifying.*

"That's what happens when you decide to panic in a dark, confined space hovering God-knows-how-many yards above the ground," he grumbles, the sting of my own words impossible to miss. "Any alpha worth his salt would lose his shit with this strong a scent of female fear."

"Oh." I don't know what to say to that. "Um... thank you?"

He barks a sharp, humorless laugh. "It's not a fucking compliment."

"Oh. Sorry." I'm pretty thankful the darkness is hiding what I'm very sure is the deepest blush of my lifetime.

But despite the impressive heights of awkwardness and the complete silence surrounding us yet again, I still feel infinitely better in his begrudging embrace than I did before.

I don't know how long we stand like that, but when I move a little to ease the beginning discomfort in my calves and accidentally lean more heavily on him, he shifts his body to take more of my weight.

"Thank you," I murmur, because it seems rude not to.

McCain grunts in response.

A few minutes later, he asks, "What's your name?"

Alarm bells at the back of my skull stop me from blurting out the answer. If I give him my actual name, I am one hundred percent getting the sack first thing tomorrow. I briefly consider telling him Rebecca Larson—the food thief who keeps stealing my packed dinner—but my conscience wins out in the end.

"Um. Bella Grayman," I lie.

"Hmm," he hums, and something about the note of it makes me think he suspects I'm not telling the truth.

"What are you doing for Christmas?" I blurt. It's such an obvious attempt at a distraction that I expect him to call me out, but before he can, the light flicks back on.

I squint against the unexpected brightness, and then

lurch forward and deeper into his chest when the elevator jolts.

McCain tightens his embrace, possibly to stop me from stomping on his expensive loafers, and I gasp an embarrassed "thank you" and dart a glance up.

He's staring at me, an unreadable expression on his stony features—but he's not letting me go, either.

Good God, he's handsome.

The thought comes from out of nowhere and is immediately followed by a rush of heat shooting first to my abdomen, then to my face.

That's when I remember the mistletoe. We're standing directly underneath it.

I've definitely watched one too many Christmas romances this year, because for the briefest of seconds, I actually think he's going to kiss me.

His eyes darken, his nostrils flare, and I *swear* he grasps me just a little closer... And then he follows my wide-eyed stare to the mistletoe right above our heads.

But when he looks back at me, it's clearly not with any sort of romance in mind. His eyebrows arc all the way to his hairline, then bunch in a frown, his soft mouth turning to a tight, angry line.

Oh, Lord no, does he think I'm trying to seduce him?

"I, uh, didn't put that there." I don't know why I say that. *I. Don't. Know.* But the words are out of my mouth before I can stop them, and if I thought sniffing him in the dark was awkward, then *oh boy,* is this an upgrade.

The alpha releases me as if burned and takes a step back, his face something resembling stony fury, and I just want the Earth to open up and swallow me whole.

But instead, a merry little *pling* interrupts the palpable tension, and the elevator doors slide open, revealing the ground floor—and two guys in blue maintenance uniforms. *Hallelujah, salvation!*

"Sir, are you all right?" one of them asks.

I don't stick around to hear the answer. Without looking back, I spin around and flee McCain Tower.

THREE
IN THE SHADOWS, ONE CHRISTMAS EVE

I nearly don't go into work the next day. If McCain's figured out who I am, I don't want to be anywhere near his damn tower. He can have me fired via email, thank you very much.

It's only the realization that a busy CEO likely won't have time to scan every employee portrait in HR's database to find the annoying woman who snuck a ride on his Elevator of Privilege that makes me get on the train to Mattenburg Central. Well, that and the need to pay my mortgage.

THERE ARE no guards waiting in the snow by the entry to McCain Enterprises to haul me up for an ass chewing. I spend the first few hours by my desk flicking between my calendar and my inbox in fear that a meeting with HR—or, horror, McCain himself—will pop up, but thankfully, nothing shows.

By the end of my shift, I'm so worn down from getting screamed at by angry customers that I finally give up worrying about any consequences of my elevator mishap. Looks like the fib about my name worked, and the CEO indeed didn't have the time or interest in hunting down a lowly employee to punish her for her misdeeds.

BY THE TIME Christmas Eve rolls around, I'm dead inside.

There is something extra-depressing about seeing the very worst of humankind during the time of year that's supposed to be filled with nothing but good tidings and love. It's not that I don't understand how frustrating it is to have put your trust in our shitty company to make your children's Christmas special, only to be let down because of a shipping error that you have no control over—but I don't, either, and it just plain sucks to be yelled at for hours on end.

I bought supplies to bake Christmas cookies earlier in the month, determined to make it happen this year, but I've not found the energy. I also had grand plans about making an actual full Christmas spread from scratch, but thankfully I gave up on that more than a week ago and just bought a frozen turkey dinner instead. By eight p.m. on the twenty-fourth, when I finally log off the Unending Stream of Fury, my only consolation is that at least I'm off until January second and don't have to deal with all the angry calls between Christmas and New Year's. December truly is the shittiest of all the months.

DESPITE MY GLOOMY MOOD, it's impossible not to notice the Christmas cheer all around me as I make my way from McCain Tower to Mattenburg Central. There are twinkling lights around every shop window and strung high across the streets in festive ribbons, and the freezing temperatures that have my breath misting in cold puffs preserve the drifts of snow lining every road.

When I pass by Town Square, where our new Lord Mayor has erected an ice-skating rink along with the traditional eighty-foot tree, I feel a suction in my gut at all the laughing families skating on the ice and admiring the tree together. I'm so envious I have to bite the inside of my cheek until I taste blood to will back tears.

I loved Christmas too, once upon a time. I still do, as proven by the fact that I always have some small hope of recreating just a little of the magic it used to have. But every year, I'm faced with the reality that December sucks and holiday cheer is for people who don't work in customer service, and/or have family who don't jet off on a cruise rather than host Christmas for their adult child. Yes, I'm a little bitter, but I don't blame my parents, really. They've got their own lives to live, and they like to spend the colder months as far south as they can get.

MY HOME IS a small townhouse on a quiet street about fifteen minutes' walk from the train station. I pop into the store on the way back for a bottle of wine, determined to have at least a half-hour soak in the tub with a glass of red and some candles to wash off a bit of the stress before bed.

The moment I turn down my road and spot my house with the wreath on the door and the chain of twinkle lights around the downstairs windows, I lose a little of the gloom.

I'm exhausted and cranky, and a little sad, but tomorrow there is no work and no demands, and sure, I might be alone, but at least there is still Christmas movies and my cozy little house with the tree I managed to decorate early in the month.

My mortgage eats up most of my salary, but it's so worth it. My home is the one place I feel entirely safe in the world, and the little jolt of happiness I get when I close the door behind me never goes away.

I put my bag down on the console table by the door

and inhale the faint scent of pine coming from my living room.

But... it doesn't smell quite *right*.

I frown into my darkened hallways. It's definitely pine-y, but there's another layer to the scent that doesn't smell like my home. I sniff again as I reach for the light switch. No, there's definitely something odd there, and though I can't put my finger on that smell, it does seem... weirdly familiar.

My fingers flick the light switch, but the hallway lamp doesn't respond.

"Shit." God, I hope it's just the bulb. I'm not sure I've got any spare fuses lying around, and even if I run, there's no way I'd make it back to the store before they close.

I fumble farther into my house and make it to the archway to my living room, where the faint light from outside illuminates the Christmas tree and part of the floor. But the twinkling lights wound around the tree that I left on before I went to work are dark. Not a good sign.

My fingers connect with the living room light switch, but any hopes I still harbored are quickly dashed; they're as dead as the hall lights.

"Dammit!" I bite my lip to will back tears of despair. It's gonna be fine. One of my neighbors will have a spare set of fuses. I just need to—

My thoughts come to an abrupt halt when a floor-board creaks behind me, and that familiar-yet-unfamiliar scent hits my nostrils with far more insistence, overpowering everything else.

Every hair on my body rises as absolute terror hits the pit of my gut.

Oh, God. Oh God, no.

I *do* recognize that smell.

I don't make it more than one step forward before a strong arm wraps around my stomach and yanks me back into a hard chest. Before I can scream, a large hand covers my mouth.

"Shh," a deep voice purrs into my ear. "There's no reason to run, my sweet. I've been waiting for you."

His smell is all around me now, deep and rich and overwhelmingly *male*—the animalic scent of alpha in rut.

And there is only one possible reason he's been waiting in the shadows for me.

FOUR
PRETTY SILK RIBBONS

I'm going to be raped.

The thought pounds in my temples and runs through my veins like acid. I shriek into his palm and flail for something, anything, to save me. My fingertips connect with the shelf by the light switch, and I manage to grab a book before he pulls me deeper into the hallway. I use it to slam as hard as I can up and back.

The alpha grunts at the impact, but I can tell I didn't hit his face like I intended.

"Feisty." He sounds more amused than anything else and plucks the book from me as easily as if I'd been a child. Before I can scratch at him, he wraps both arms around my body, securing me against his bulk. "You don't need to fight me, Eve. You won't come to any harm in my hands."

He knows my name. Jesus Christ, does that mean the psycho's been stalking me?

I suck in a lungful of air, but before I can let out a scream, he puts one hand over my mouth again while keeping my body immobilized with his other arm.

"I'm sorry you're scared," he murmurs against my hair. And then he nuzzles at it affectionately, as if we're longtime lovers. Rubs his cheek against my scalp and squeezes my body as if to soothe my trembling. "But I promise you'll be okay."

Super comforting, coming from the psychopath who's broken into my home. I don't wait for him to say anything else—I smack my head back and right into his face.

His grunt is slightly more pained this time, but my efforts do nothing to loosen his grip. When I aim a kick at his shins, he only sighs, easily moving his leg out of range.

I scream into his hand again, frustration mixing with the terror and blind panic. I twist, strain, claw, stomp, and *scream*—anything to hurt him, anything to get even the smallest moment to escape—but it's all for nothing.

I fight for nearly half an hour, until I have nothing left to give and the last vestiges of adrenaline are burned out of my system.

Only when I sag against him with a defeated whine does he finally loosen his hold ever-so slightly.

"Are you done?" He's not even out of breath.

The tears come then, on the heels of the undeniable

understanding that there is nothing I can do to escape this. He will have me, and I can't stop him.

"Shh, don't cry," he murmurs, his deep rumble softening as he releases his hold on my mouth to wipe a stray tear from my cheek. "I don't want you to cry."

"Don't hurt me." It comes out in a pitiful blubber.

"I won't harm you, Eve. You have my word," he says, and I desperately try to find some solace in the absolute sincerity in his voice, even if the distinction he makes doesn't go unnoticed. I've never been with an alpha, but I know enough about their anatomy to realize that what he wants from me, even if I walk away unharmed... it *will* hurt.

At my renewed crying, the intruder spins me around to rest my face against his chest, cradling the back of my head with a large hand. But instead of more meaningless words of reassurance, he purrs.

"*Oh.*" I blink into his black sweater, confusion muddling my thoughts. It's a low, rich rumble that seems to emanate from all around me and penetrate deep into my bones, and I've never heard anything like it. Sure, I've seen a few movies with a purring alpha, but nothing —*nothing*—can compare to this.

Every muscle in my exhausted body softens, and my breathing slows as my mind fogs into blissful nothingness.

I never knew anything could feel this... this *safe*. My

fear is gone as if it never existed. There is nothing but pleasure.

Warm hands stroke down the length of my back, rubbing small circles against my spine before he smooths his palm back up to my nape over and over, until I feel nothing but his strong muscles and that all-enveloping alpha warmth. His scent is heavy in my nostrils, heady and rich, and *oh*, I could *bathe* in it. Deep and musky and *male*.

I rub against his chest, mindless to anything but the need for more of his delicious musk, and moan softly when his purr pitches deeper in obvious approval. *Oh, yes, that's even better.*

Soft lips brush against my scalp, my temple, the shell of my ear, and when I press deeper into him for more, something hard rises against my belly.

On some distant plane, I recognize that this—this is the part where I should find the strength to keep fighting. But his purr keeps the terror of what's going to happen next at bay. Instead, warmth pools low in my abdomen and I feel myself... *soften*.

"*Oh*." It's a coo, soft and feminine, and unlike any sound I've made before.

"That's it," he purrs. "It'll feel so, so good, my sweet. Give in."

"Mmm," I agree, rubbing my nose deeper into his

sweater until he brushes a couple of fingers underneath my jaw to tip my head up.

He's wearing a black balaclava with two openings for his eyes and mouth, and in the darkness, I can't even make out his eye color. My stomach tightens at the visual reminder that this is a stranger, an intruder—

"Shh." Warm lips dip for mine, and the spark of unease drowns in the taste of his mouth.

Oh, God, I've never been kissed like this.

He devours my mouth slow and deep, flicking his tongue at my lips until I part them on instinct, and he's *inside.* We both groan. Mine is high-pitched, his low and deep. He clutches at my hips, then reaches for my ass to lift me.

I part my knees for him, too lost in the kiss and his unwavering purr to worry when he wraps my legs around his waist and closes his arms around me, then heads for the stairs.

And how could I worry? Every inch of my skin is warm from the heat he radiates, every breath laced with his rich aroma and intoxicating flavor. My pulse throbs steadily down low, a delicious sort of itch spreading through my body, and that *purr—oh,* it's both soothing and exciting, calling out to something primal I didn't know I contained. *This is where you belong,* it seems to say. *This is where you're safe.*

When he puts me down on the floor again, I mewl unhappily into his mouth.

He chuckles softly, his breath wafting over me as he pulls back with a few scorching kisses to my jaw. "Patience, beautiful."

I plaster myself to his body and stretch up, eager for his lips to return to mine, but he grabs my shoulders and spins me around without acquiescing to my demands.

I blink in dazed confusion. He's taken me to my bedroom.

Soft, flickering light from several white pillar candles scattered around the room lets me see he's changed the sheets and stacked my pillows by the headboard. Red, silky ribbons—scarves, from the looks of them—are tied to the wrought metal.

"You... prepared this?" I mumble. Alarm tries to claw its way past the blissful fog slowing my brain, but his purr vibrates unrelentingly through my back, making it impossible to think.

"I did." He brushes my hair over my shoulder and kisses the side of my neck, then grips my sweater and eases it over my head. "Every moment, I've thought about how I would take you. When I slept, my dreams were of nothing but the raw, carnal desperation to be inside of you, but by *day*... I planned."

The alpha kisses my neck again and unhooks my bra,

and my nipples instantly tighten at the first touch of cool air.

"No one's ever called to me like you, little temptress. I'm afraid you've made me quite mad with yearning," he whispers before reaching for my zipper. "Every time you passed the alley by the station, all I could think about was dragging you in and having you against the wall like a brute. But I couldn't do that. Not to you. Just the thought of you disrespected like that..."

His voice dips to a threatening growl, purr momentarily stuttering out. I tense on instinct at the aggressive sound, but before the spell fully lifts from my confused mind, he ghosts a breath against my ear and resumes the purring, louder than before. When I sag back against him, he eases my pants over my hips and then hooks his fingers in the waistband of my panties to slide them down as well. When they pool at my feet, he lifts me back up, bridal-style.

I look up at him, and am met with a gaze so full of heat I have to squeeze my thighs together to stop a trickle of liquid from escaping. Oh, but he looks like he wants to *devour* me.

He crosses the floor to my bed in two steps and kneels on the mattress to place me in the center. "The first time I met you, I was so angry with you. I was perfectly content in life, and then suddenly, there you were. Making me *want.* Do you know what that's like, my sweet? To want until your soul aches?"

The alpha guides my left hand to my headboard and carefully wraps one silk scarf around my wrist. When he's done, he tests the binding with a finger, ensuring it's not too tight, before he straddles me to reach for my other wrist.

"But there is no point in hating you," he continues. "Not when what I crave is so easily taken."

"I—wait. Please, I..." What he says... I try to focus on the intent overlaying the deep purr. His tone is indulgent and laced with heat that makes my pussy throb, but the words are sinister enough to pierce the veil of contentment.

"No. I won't wait any longer, Eve. I can't." He fastens my right wrist and kisses my palm while I stare at him with parted lips, caught in the warm maelstrom of his purr and the hot pulse of my own body. "And deep down, you can't, either. I smell you, my sweet. You want this too."

I do want this—*him.* Unease momentarily forgotten, I watch him through hooded eyes as he rolls off me and grabs me under my left knee. A sharp zing of excitement burns through the calm lethargy at the feel of his hand so tantalizingly close to my weeping pussy, and I tilt my pelvis up on instinct.

"Needy little thing." His smile is feral. Slowly he pulls my thigh up and out, then reaches for another of the ribbons tied to my headboard. This one's longer, but when he wraps it right above my knee, the stretch is harsh. I wiggle on the bed to ease the strain on my muscles, but he places a hand on my hip and stills my movements.

"Shh, you'll be okay," he promises, voice smooth and rumbly with his purr, but the discomfort of the stretch helps me focus my foggy thoughts. Something... something is not okay.

"Why are you doing this?" I protest. I try to reach for the scarf around my thigh, but my arms stay by the side of my head thanks to the bindings. Real dread finally nestles in my gut. "Please, what are you—?"

My voice dies on a sharp inhale when the alpha moves his hand from my hip to my mound and pushes his thumb to my hooded clit.

Electricity sparks through my pelvis, and when he rubs his thumb up and down, I throw my head back onto the pillows and groan, hazy alarm drowned in the rush of pleasure crackling through my nerves. *Shit, that feels so good!*

A rough growl vibrates through the alpha's purr, and liquid heat floods from my pussy at the sound.

He sucks in a breath and lets out a suffering groan.

"I'm going to bury my tongue in you and drink until you've got no more left to give." He snarls it like a threat, but it only makes me whimper and my pussy contract as he rubs the hood of my clit with increasingly maddening firmness.

But instead of following through, he removes his hand from my thrumming clit and grabs for the scarf again.

"No, please, *more*," I protest, tugging desperately on my arms in a futile attempt at taking over what he abandoned. But though he's ensured the bindings are not so tight they cut off circulation, there is no give in them either.

The alpha ignores my pleas. His mouth is slanted in a grim line, and his focus is on the red scarf as he winds it a couple more times around my thigh. Then he brushes a hand down my leg, pulls my woolen sock off, and grabs me by the ankle to guide my calf up tight against my thigh.

He's no longer purring, and though my body throbs with echoes of the attention he paid my clit, the fog finally begins to clear.

"W-what are you doing?" I croak as he winds the scarf around my bent leg below the knee, securing it with several loops.

"I am opening you." His voice is pure gravel. It makes my clit pang, but there is nothing comforting about it. When he moves to grab my other leg, instincts that should have been present all along kick in, and I try to jerk away, but it's too late—much, much too late.

He easily catches my flailing limb and loops the final

ribbon around my thigh, then pulls it tight until I am open in a hundred-and-eighty-degree angle. The strain on my groin and inner thigh muscles finally lifts the last remnants of calm. Absolute terror takes its place.

I've let a stranger strip me and tie me up.

"You see, I am going to do such delicious things to your pretty little pussy," he says. He pulls the sock off my right foot and kisses the sole before securing that leg against my thigh like he did the other, leaving me entirely powerless. "Over. And over. And over. If I gave you a choice in the matter, you might try to deny me before I've had my fill. And we can't have that, now can we, Eve?"

He pulls back to kneel between my forcefully splayed legs, and I see him for what he is—clad in all black and with his face hidden behind a mask: an intruder, here to *take*.

FIVE
MISTLETOE BARGAIN

"No, no, please, no!" I pull desperately on my bindings, but he clearly knows what he's doing. They don't give so much as an inch.

"Shh, there's no need to be frightened. A moment ago you wanted this, remember?" With a casualness that seems almost insulting, given the situation, he shrugs out of his black sweater.

I've never seen a man like him. His pecs are thick with muscle and *wide*, his shoulders massive, and the span of his biceps is thicker than my thighs. His abs look like they're sculpted from marble.

He is the absolute epitome of power—and I am help-less before him.

Hunger blazes in his gaze as his eyes roam over my

body. When they land between my splayed legs, a rich growl rumbles out of his chest.

A trickle of moisture seeps out of me at that sound, even as I whimper with fear. Despite myself, my pussy softens at the knowledge that nothing and no one can stop this man from taking what he wants.

Panic rips a sob from my throat, and in desperation I plead, "Please, please just stop. If-if you leave now, I won't go to the police, I promise."

The alpha's expression turns serious and softens ever-so slightly. "Don't go to the police, Eve; they do bad things to women crying alpha rape without visible injuries. I won't have that happen to you."

I've heard the rumors, but I always thought them an urban legend. The expression in the intruder's eyes tells me I've been very, very wrong.

Without warning, I begin to cry. Great, heaping sobs of despair.

A rumble escapes the alpha's throat. It's a noise of discontent. "Stop crying. I told you I won't harm you."

His words do nothing to stop my flood of tears. He purrs, then, that same, deep rumbling sound that quelled my frightened cries before. It sinks into my nervous system and lulls my fear enough for the tears to slowly stop, but the despair remains as a dark cloud. I look at him with red-rimmed eyes.

"Please," I whisper. "Let me go."

His purr cuts out and he leans back on his heels. "Dammit!" He rubs his hand over his masked face. "How do you fucking do this to me?"

I want to point out that, being the one trussed up like a holiday turkey, I'm not *doing* anything, but I'm not dumb enough to argue with an agitated alpha who has me at his mercy.

He shoots me something close to a glare, then sighs deeply, his tense posture easing a little. "All right. Here's what we're gonna do, Eve. You say... hm, 'mistletoe,' and I'll stop. I'll untie you. And I'll leave—"

"Mistletoe!" I immediately croak.

The alpha gives me an admonishing look. "Be a good girl and listen to the rest of my offer. If it's still 'mistletoe,' then I'll honor my promise. But I suspect you might reconsider."

I blink at him. "O-offer?"

"Yes, Eve. Offer." He lets out another, more annoyed sigh. "I've never been one to hold back from taking what I want, but you... Your tears are... unsettling. So instead of simply taking what's mine, I'll buy it."

"*Buy* it?" I croak, immediately incensed. "You think I'm a whore?!"

"No, baby girl, I don't." He strokes up one of my restrained thighs and ghosts his thumb up the seam of my slippery pussy lips. I shiver in my bindings at his touch, unwanted pleasure cutting deep as he grazes my clit.

"But everyone has a price. Now, let's see if I can't find yours...

"You work as a customer rep, making just above minimum wage, but you own this house. Based on the information I could find and the low cost of everything else you own, your mortgage takes up most of your budget. So here's my offer, Eve: You let me have you for the night —the whole night—without using your safe word, and in return, when the banks open on the 27th, I'll pay off your house. You will own it in full—no more mortgage, no more scraping by. Yours."

I gape up at him, struggling to fully comprehend the magnitude of his offer. "M-my mortgage? You're saying you'll pay off my *entire* mortgage, if I...?"

"Yes. That's how much your pussy's worth to me." He moves the pad of his thumb over my clit again, a little more deliberately this time. "One night of opening your sweet little cunt for me, and you will never risk homelessness again."

I jerk against my bonds at the stimulation, my breath coming out in a sharp exhale. Despite my reluctance, my body responds to him like a finely tuned violin, the shock of his touch making it hard to think. "Y-you've got that kind of money? More than two hundred and fifty *thousand* dollars? For *one* night? Why not buy an actual sex worker?"

"Yes, Eve, I've got that kind of money." He leans

forward, piercing me with his gaze, letting me see the absolute sincerity in its depths. "What I need from you is not a *fuck*, baby girl, and it can't be bought on a street corner. I want every ounce of you, every molecule of your body, your mind. You may scream and sob and fight—but in the end, you'll surrender to the pleasure, painful as it may prove. *That's* what I need. And you're the only one who can give it to me. So, my sweet little thing... do we have a deal?"

I stare up at him, still terrified out of my mind and unable to ignore the slow circles he's drawing on my clit. But... he's offering to pay my *mortgage*. Without that monthly expense, I could breathe again. I could even save up for school, go back and retrain, get a job that doesn't involve being screamed at.

God, am I seriously considering this? Am I going to let myself get fucked by a stranger, an *alpha*, for money? Granted, it's *a lot* of money—enough that I could make a better life for myself. The price is one night of pain. Just one.

I bite my lip against the sensations buzzing through my body. It feels good; I don't want it to, but it does. My pulse throbs in my veins, heavy and fast, racing from the unrelenting rubbing of my bud of nerves and the full, rich scent of alpha in rut.

There's no guarantee he's telling the truth—he could easily trick me, have his fill, and leave me aching and used without a penny. But if that were his intention, why didn't he just rape me as he had planned? Why go through this charade? Why negotiate and cajole when he's already proven he can easily take what he wants without the pretense of consent?

My terror eases the tiniest bit as I look up into his darkened gaze. He's negotiating because the sight of my tears was enough to derail his carefully laid plans. He knows where I work, what I earn, what my mortgage costs —he's stalked me, observed my habits, prepared in every conceivable way for this one night. And yet my tears brought it all crashing down.

That knowledge shouldn't calm me as much as it does. Still, I hear myself asking, "You'll stop? At any point? If I... If I say 'mistletoe'?"

He nods without breaking eye contact. "At any point before penetration. Once I'm inside you... there won't be a power in this world strong enough to make me stop."

My lips tremble, my heart rate picking up speed again. "W-what if it hurts too bad? What if—"

"I won't harm you, Eve," he says, his voice soft despite the gravel of lust. "It's not about the pain—I'll do every- thing I can to prepare you, to make it tolerable. You won't bleed. And everything that comes before that point—I'll make you feel things you never knew you could. The chemistry between us... I know you feel it too. Your pussy is gushing for me already. I'll make you come until you don't care how badly it hurts when I force my cock inside you.

"Let me show you how good it can feel to surrender your body, baby girl. Then I'll make your pretty little pussy work off your mortgage, and we'll go our separate ways." He gives me a smirk. "Perhaps limping, in your case, but with a $257,000 increase to your net worth."

Shit, I'm actually considering this. If only he'd stop rubbing my clit so I could get my brain back under control! But... two hundred and fifty-seven *thousand* dollars... And, oh *God,* his thumb on my pulsing bud of nerves feels so good!

Muted, as if the sound comes through water, I hear myself whisper, "Okay."

A slow, dangerous smirk pulls on the corner of the intruder's mouth, and despite my agreement, another shiver of terror crawls up my spine.

"Very good, baby girl," he purrs, the softness gone from his voice as his predatory gaze slips back down between my splayed thighs. "Now, let's get a closer look at what I bought."

SIX
A PERFECTLY WRAPPED PRESENT

I suck in a hard breath and pull on my bindings in an instinctive attempt to hide my most intimate parts from the alpha's hungry eyes, but he clearly knows what he's doing; the silk scarves remain unyielding.

"Don't be frightened. It'll feel so, so good in a minute." He inhales deeply, the sound ending on a groan. *"God."* When he leans in over me, placing a hand on each side of my ribs so he can stare into my eyes, my breath stutters in my throat. I thought I knew desire, but the absolute blaze of this man's lust burns like a firestorm. When he has had his fill, will there be anything left of me?

"You make me mad, woman. You make me *ache.*" He falls on top of me, the heat of his bare skin against mine an unexpected comfort, even as he settles heavily between my bound legs and my abdomen clenches with trepidation.

The intruder drags his nose up along my jaw to the side of my neck, his deep inhale ending on a growl. "I'll make you ache too, sweet one," he rasps into my ear.

"Please. Please be gentle," I whimper, even though I know that's not what he wants. That's not what I agreed to.

"Gentle?" His breath teases over my sensitive skin, raising goosebumps and tightening my nipples. And my clit. He nudges my chin with a finger, turning my head to catch my eyes. Behind the mask, his gaze is pure animal dominance—an alpha relishing his control. "I smell you, Eve—your pussy. You're so wet for me you're soaking the sheets. You need this as bad as I do, need it just as rough."

Shame flames my cheeks because I know he's right— my entire body is thrumming for him, every drum of my pulse throbbing hard in my clit and making my opening quiver for penetration. For his dominance.

"No," I lie.

He chuffs a rough chuckle and presses a hot kiss to my lips that leaves my mouth tingling. "Your body knows me, darling. It's biology. You were born for my cock, and your pussy knows it. But don't worry—before I'm done with you, you'll have learned to listen to her."

With that, he bends his head for my throat, teeth digging in hard enough to shoot a spike of animalistic panic through my brain before he softens his bite and sucks wetly at my pulse point.

When he pulls back, he's panting hard. "Fuck, how are you doing this? One taste of your skin, and all I can think about is—" He bites back whatever else he was going to say. Snarling, he buries his mouth in my breasts.

His hot lips close around one stiff nipple, immediately followed by wet, deep suction. I jerk in my bindings and cry out at the bolt of lightning shooting straight to my clit. He rumbles approvingly and flicks my nipple with his tongue before delving a hand down between my thighs, heading straight for my clit.

I jolt again at the direct touch to my sensitive nub; my forced arousal has made the small organ to protrude past its protective hood. "*Shit!* No! No, please, not there!"

I babble the plea out even as my body sings at finally receiving stimulation where it needs it most, because *fuck,* it's too direct, too *much,* and if he keeps rubbing me there, I know with absolute certainty that I'll *break.* His fingers are firm and unrelenting, drawing sharp little circles across the tip without any preamble, driving me toward a peak my mind refuses to accept.

"Stop! God, please *stop!*" I beg, pulling frantically on my ties. It's no use; I'm completely immobilized, entirely at his mercy, and he has none.

Easing off my nipple, he rasps, "You need this, my sweet. If you want it to stop, you know what to do. Give me your safe word and relinquish the money, or gush that little pussy for me."

I howl when he dives for my other breast and sucks my nipple deep into the cavern of his mouth, fingers turning vicious on my clit. But I need that money.

There's nothing I can do; my body is not mine to control. It's his, and I am quickly learning that there is no denying him. My climax rises like fire through my thighs, tightening my muscles in preparation for the inevitable. I fall off the cliff still crying in denial.

"No, no, no, n—*oooh!*"

Everything is heat and tight, too-intense pleasure. My pussy flutters in hard little cramps, forcing me to arch against his evil fingers continuing to rub sensation into my overstimulated clit. My nipples are tight points, one still deep in his mouth, and every pull on it forces another shudder of release through my quaking pelvis.

"P-please," I moan again. "Please, *please.*"

Miraculously, he listens. Those hellish fingertips soften, easing me down from the edge of madness with gentle strokes that gradually lighten. When he finally moves from my clitoris to tease a finger through my soaking folds, I am boneless beneath him.

A rough growl rumbles through the alpha, rich and deep. He lifts off me, popping his mouth off my glistening nipple to rake his gaze over my face and down my body to between my thighs. Despite my more than sated state, my pussy flutters weakly at the heat of his attention.

It's all the warning I get before he trails a finger down the seam of my lips and then pushes it up inside me.

"*Oh!*" It doesn't hurt—I'm much too wet for that—but I'm unprepared for intrusion, and the man has big hands.

His eyelids flutter shut at the sound of my sharp moan, a harsh breath escaping his own lips. Slowly he draws the finger halfway out, only to push it back up before it can slip out. "What I wouldn't give to be inside you this very second."

I frown, doing my best to ignore the slow fingering. What in the world does he mean? He could have me if he wanted to—my submission to the rough orgasm he just forced from me should have shown him I'm desperate enough to do everything in my power not to use my safe word. In fact, I don't know why he's taking the time to prepare me like this. My pussy was wet and shamelessly eager even before he began playing with my clit, and *now?* His slow pumps into me make embarrassing, slick sounds that speak all too clearly of my body's complete surrender.

I don't voice my confusion—he might see it as encouragement, and though my pussy might be ready for what comes next, I'm not.

He slips another finger into me, making me gasp at the unexpected stretch. *Shit,* he really does have big hands!

His lip twitches at my sharp exhale. "It feels good

when I stretch you, doesn't it, baby girl? And there's so much more to come."

The shock of his fingertips digging directly into my G-spot makes me bow up against the ribbons tying me down. When he begins rubbing it, I'm entirely incapable of holding back a long, broken moan.

"That's it," he rasps. "*Fuck,* that's it. All I want is to make you feel so, *so* good. Be a good girl and cream for me. That's it. Just like that."

Why is my pussy responding to his filthy words? For every pump of his fingers, I feel my body wake from the numb aftershocks of my first orgasm, my fried nerve endings sparking with the first buzzes of pleasure. The sloshing sounds emitting from my sheath are even louder than before.

He fingers me until I am panting rhythmically, and my hands fist in my bonds every time he spreads his fingers apart to open me a little wider. Then, without warning, he pulls his hand from my pussy, leaving me empty.

I whine at the loss before I can stop myself.

The intruder smirks and holds his fingers up between us. They're dripping with my fluids. "You *are* a good girl, aren't you? Creaming for your alpha to show him how much you need him. You'd let me fuck you even without the money, wouldn't you?"

"N-no." It comes out a breathless moan—needy, even to my own ears.

He stares at me, daring me to deny the evidence coating his fingers in thick strings. My face heats, the proof of my pussy's eagerness scalding my cheeks with shame.

With another smirk, he brings his fingers to his mouth and sucks them clean.

The second my cream touches his tongue, a snarl rips from the big male. His eyes squeeze shut, and a tremor moves through his powerful body. When he opens his eyes again, they are void of anything but black animal instinct. Despite my body's hum, terror tightens my spine in response. Right now, there is nothing remotely human about it—and I am trapped before him, tied open like a sacrificial lamb.

Roaring, he lunges.

SEVEN

AN ORC COMES FOR CHRISTMAS

I whimper and brace for pain—but pain is not what he's after.

His large hands land on my inner thighs as he throws himself down between my bound legs, immediately sliding up to my pussy to roughly part my labia, baring me completely.

I only manage to gasp before he pulls up his mask, presses his face into my still-sopping sex, and *sucks*.

I shriek and moan despite myself when his tongue plunges deep into my slit and slides down to my opening.

He groans like a wounded beast and drinks my fluids like a man dying from thirst, the sounds he pulls from my pussy wet and obscene. A hazy thought that I finally get why it's called *"eating pussy"* flickers through my brain, but is swiftly forgotten as he thrusts his tongue up inside my hole for more.

Shit, that shouldn't feel good! The wet squelching sounds so dirty and *wrong,* but my clit throbs with every stroke of his tongue, and *fuck, fuck, fuck,* he needs to stop!

"No! Stop! *Stop!*" I cry out the words, but they don't sound convincing in the slightest, all breathy and hoarse.

The intruder only growls at me, the sound reverberating through my pussy and into my pelvis—and then he shifts his mouth from my opening to my clit.

If I thought getting my nipples sucked was maddening, it's nothing—*nothing*—compared to the sheer seismic insanity that rips through my entire nervous system when he closes his lips around my clit and *pulls.*

My nub, still swollen and exposed from my orgasm, disappears deep into his hot mouth—and my world explodes into crippling *sensation.* There is pleasure, somewhere past the screaming of every nerve in my body, but mostly it feels *too much,* and I writhe and scream and fight my bonds, reduced to a quivering mass of flesh and instincts.

"*No, no, no, nooooo!*" I come so hard I see stars, howling in denial even as my pussy spasms rhythmically around a rush of ecstasy more powerful than any I've had before.

Too much. Too much. The words echo in my foggy

brain, like some ominous threat of seizure from my nervous system even as my body still throbs through its climax. But even when my pleasure ebbs I'm allowed no rest.

His lips are merciless, the suction on my now spent and hypersensitive clit relentless, and the satiation of release quickly flicks to raw, grating overstimulation.

"N-no. Please," I rasp, trying to shift my pelvis to dislodge the man. "Please, stop, please. It's too much!"

He growls in response and sucks me harder, flicking his tongue against my quivering clit as if punishing my attempt at severing him from my pussy.

It feels like a whiplash, and I cry out wordlessly and throw my head back against the pillow, fists clenching against the roar of sensation. Again, he flicks my clit, his wet tongue wrapping around the suspended pearl forcing raw, brutal stimulation through the trembling organ and right to my brainstem.

I try to gasp another plea for mercy, but before my mouth can shape the words, my mind goes blank.

I have no comprehension of time. One minute I'm floating in white nothingness—the next I'm once more drowning in heat and firing nerves. I gasp a protest, bracing against the expected torment, but... it feels almost good now; warm and rhythmic stimulation forcing me toward another peak.

I grit my teeth and rock back against his mouth, determined to ride the wave of pleasure rather than get sucked back under by the torrents.

The sounds he makes help—dirty, wet sucking and deep groans of enjoyment drive spikes of exhilaration through my pelvis. His desire for me is so indisputable, so entirely blunt and unapologetic, I can't help my body's instinctive response. I've never been wanted—no, *needed* —like this, and it makes some twisted, submissive part of my brain want to give him everything he demands.

"Okay. Okay." I'm only half-aware of my breathy babbles, my entire focus trapped on my pulsing clit. I clench my hands and squeeze my eyes shut, and focus on the rhythm of the suction—those deep, harsh pulls that go all the way to the root; the tease of his tongue against the tip... *Fuck!*

"*Y-yes!*" I wail out my orgasm, hands flexing with instinctive urge to grab onto the source of my pleasure as warm, perfect relief floods through my pelvis, up my spine and down my thighs, leaving my mind blissfully numb to anything but ecstasy for several frantic heartbeats.

When I collapse in a heap of spent nerves and thrumming flesh, he finally—*finally*—eases off my clit and pushes back up to his knees.

I watch him through hooded lids, too exhausted to feel anything but acceptance at what I know comes next. I'm entirely spent, my desire for sex sated beyond what I knew to be possible, but I know I will have to take him inside of me now. His eyes flame black from pure, animalistic *need* as he stares at my splayed and soaking pussy, his wide chest heaving with his labored breaths. Why he isn't on top of me already, rutting like a wild beast, I don't understand.

"Fuck." He groans the word, his deep voice tormented, and leans back in over me. But instead of settling his bulk between my thighs, he reaches across the bed for my nightstand.

Wha—? My muddled brain doesn't finish the question before he pulls out a heavy length of silicone—and despite my exhausted state, I flush with mortification.

Along with a wand vibrator, I own two dildos. One is perfectly proper; purple, smooth, slim. It's what I use on nights I need some relief.

The other...

The other is the result of drinking too much wine while reading a particularly spicy Asian webcomic late at night. When it arrived in the mail a week later, I opened the discreet box it shipped in, laughed myself silly, and put it away at the bottom of my closet, untouched.

According to the manufacturer, it's "the orc chieftain's mightiest weapon." It's green, it's rudely detailed, and it's so ridiculously huge I had to pay an absolute fortune in shipping. I can't even close my hand around the damn thing, and in the bright light of sobriety, I had absolutely no intention of putting it anywhere near my poor vagina.

However, the fact that it's made it from my closet to my nightstand means the intruder has other plans.

My mortification shifts to unease as I eye the monstrosity. It looks less absurdly big in his oversized hand, but it's still as thick as his wrist.

"Please don't—not that," I rasp. "It's too big."

The alpha huffs a breath through his nose and moves the ridiculous toy down, aiming its blunt head at my flushed opening. Ignoring my protests entirely.

"No, no, please, I'm serious! I've never taken it before —it's too big. You'll hurt me!" I squirm on the bed, desperately trying to avoid what I know comes next, but the ribbons keep me in place, unrelenting as ever. "Please, just —just have me yourself. Don't use that, please! Use... Use your... cock. Please, it'll feel so much better for you too, right?"

Begging him for his dick is humiliating on an entirely new level, but I'm too desperate to avoid "the Chieftain" to care.

The alpha snorts again and slips two fingers deep into my pussy. He pumps them a few times, and I moan despite myself. When he pulls his digits back out, they're glossy with my juices.

He wipes my wetness over the head of the dildo and pushes it to my splayed lower lips.

"Don't worry, baby girl. You'll get my cock more times than you can stand. But first, your sweet little pussy needs to learn how to open."

And with that, he shoves the phallus through my opening.

EIGHT
BIG GREEN TREE TRUNK

"Nnggghhh!"

My pussy stretches desperately around the head of the monstrosity, my sheath burning with the effort of opening wide enough—but somehow, I take it.

"F-Fuck!" I stare down between my spread thighs, panting hard as I take in the obscenity of that thick phallus sunk a few inches deep. The hugeness of it *inside* of me looks as impossible as it feels. My thighs shake with the strain of taking it, and my entrance *aches*.

"That's a good girl." The alpha's voice is a rich rumble, the sound of it forcing a trickle of moisture from my stuffed core—as if my body responds to his dark need on instinct alone. "Nice and easy now. Open that pussy for me, Eve."

"No! *Shit—ahh!*" My protest turns to a high-pitched

keening when the intruder puts weight behind his hand—and slowly shoves the Chieftain home.

"Shit, shit, shit!" I thrash in my bindings, fists clenching and unclenching in useless protest, but there's nothing I can do to stop the merciless advance. My pussy is wet and warm from the intruder's ministrations, and even though it *shouldn't fit,* even though it burns and aches and my clit pops out obscenely from the pressure, my body slowly, inescapably yields.

I wail wretchedly when, in the end, my pussy betrays me and sucks up the last several inches with an embarrassing wet slurp, nestling the silicone mammoth right against my trembling cervix.

Conquered.

I pant hard and let my head fall back against the pillow, bracing. There is nothing more I can do. It's in so deep, my body finally recognizes the futility of resistance. Slick, inner muscles trembling from the brutal stretch clench, encouraging a mating as if I were penetrated by the male himself, not a piece of silicone.

Immediate pangs of raw sensation make me cry out. There's a deep, dull ache of being wrenched too wide, but underneath—*pleasure.* Sheer, feminine delight at being *opened* and *taken* from instincts too primitive to know the difference between an actual man and the humiliating sex toy shoved deep into my core.

"Shh, don't cry, baby girl." His voice softens, and only

when he reaches up with his free hand to wipe at the moisture from the corners of my eyes do I notice the tears trickling down my temples. When I whimper in response, he shifts on the bed to rest his massive body on top of mine, bracing his weight on one elbow. His other hand still holds the end of the dildo, ensuring the girthy behemoth stays lodged in me.

"I'm sorry it has to be like this," he murmurs against my ear, and to my surprise, he sounds sincere. "All I want is to bring you pleasure, Eve, I promise. Relax your pussy —it'll be easier to take."

Easy for him to say—he's not the one opened so wide it feels like his innermost is bared for all to see.

"I don't want this," I whine.

"I know you don't." His voice is still gentle, but any delusions I may have had that he will spare me die when he pulls the dildo halfway out of me, only to return it all the way in in a thrust far too firm to harbor any compassion.

"Ah!" I cry out and jerk at the ruthless sensation. Every nerve ending in my pussy flares to life, and then he thrusts again—and I can't take it, I can't, I can't—

"Stop! No!" I howl and thrash, desperate and panicked, but unless I'm willing to give up two hundred and fifty-seven thousand goddamn dollars, there is no way out; there's nothing I can do to spare my innermost from the impossible penetration.

He pushes the dildo deep again and brushes his lips against the shell of my ear, raising goosebumps along my arms even as my entire focus is on the burn between my thighs. "Smell me," he rumbles, the gentleness from before overshadowed by unmistakable lust now. "It'll help it feel good."

What? I'm too out of it to fully process his words, but when he shifts on the bed to pull my face into his neck, instincts take over, and I inhale a shaky breath of his heady pheromones.

"*O-oh.*" My body's response is instant. Heat floods my skin and softens my muscles. God, he smells so good. I suck in a deeper breath of his scent, and groan despite myself when the heat in my body centers in my core.

The next thrust of the dildo is easier to take. It's still much too big, the sensation of penetration too intense, but despite myself, my pussy softens ever-so slightly for every greedy lungful of alpha scent. Soon my miserable wails turn to throaty grunts, even as I still clench my fists and thrash in protest of the fucking.

"That's it," the intruder groans as he shoves the dildo home even harder. My pussy smacks wetly in response, betraying my forced pleasure as much as my keen at the increase in pace. "God, you sound so perfect. I want to be inside you so bad. I want to feel your little cunt suck on me more than I want to fucking breathe, Eve. How are you this goddamn perfect?"

For the life of me, I don't know why his filthy words bore into my skull and fog my brain with yearning for exactly that—for his cock—but *oh,* they do. Images of the big brute shoving his warm, eager member deep inside of me burns through my body, and I moan and arch into the dildo's brutal thrusts.

"Yeah, that's it, darling. Take it just like that. You were fucking born for this. Open that pussy."

He pumps the dildo faster, making me cry out, but despite the brutality, despite an edge of pain from being forced so wide still lingering behind the endorphins, my body eagerly obeys. It's not long before the fire in my core deepens, the spiral of pleasure tightening.

I've never had a vaginal orgasm before, but I know it's coming as I curve upward as much as I can in my bindings and clench down on instinct alone.

It's a mistake. When my muscles clamp around the intrusion to prepare for climax, I am brutally reminded of just how impossibly *thick* this cursed thing is.

"Ow! Fuck!" My pussy flutters desperately in a futile attempt at easing off the insertion and sparing me the agony, but it's far too late.

Growling, the alpha pumps me with hard, forceful strokes, and there's nothing I can do to stop the roar of orgasm flooding through my pelvis until—

"S-shit! *Yes!*"

Everything is heat and pleasure too intense to contain.

I curl up as much as the ribbons will allow, crying out in mindless ecstasy as my pussy massages the silicone monstrosity in tight, pulsing cramps. And then—*relief*.

I collapse down on the mattress on the ebb of orgasm, every muscle in my body nearly liquifying in the wake of it. I've never come so hard in my entire goddamn life.

Panting with exhaustion, I squint down my body to where the Chieftain is lodged deep in my core, the alpha mercifully holding it still now. It looks obscene, the way my pussy has to gape to accommodate its ridiculous girth, but it doesn't hurt anymore. My sheath, relaxed from orgasm, finally accepts the insertion.

I let my head fall back down on the pillow and close my eyes, intent on basking in the blissful haze of dopamine pulsing through my system in lazy waves.

But the alpha doesn't allow me to rest for long.

With a deep slurping sound, the intruder pulls the dildo from my drooling pussy. I moan in protest, but the bliss of it popping free is nearly as good as coming.

There's a heavy *thunk* when he tosses it aside and it hits the floor, followed by the unmistakable rattling of a belt buckle opening. He's not done with me yet.

Reluctantly, I open my eyes and try to prepare my exhausted body for more. I knew this was coming—from the moment I felt his arms around me and his erection hard and eager against my back, I knew there was only one way this night would end. No alpha breaks into a woman's house simply to pleasure *her*.

Only nothing could have prepared me for the sight that meets me when he pushes down his black pants and his cock finally springs free.

I feel the blood drain from my face as genuine terror tightens my throat, chasing away my peaceful, post-orgasmic haze.

"M-Mistletoe!"

NINE
OPENING HIS GIFT

"Eve—"

"Mistletoe, mistletoe, *mistletoe!*" The word spills past my lips in a frantic chant, my eyes glued to the monstrosity rising hard and proud between the alpha's thighs and up past his navel.

I'm not entirely innocent—I've watched my share of alpha porn. I know they're absurdly big. I've even had a couple of shameful comes to clips of some poor actress getting knotted.

But nothing—*nothing*—could have prepared me for this man's size. He's bigger than anything I've seen on even the darkest corners of the internet, twice the girth of the Chieftain, and there's absolutely no way I can take that without being broken apart. There just isn't.

The intruder groans, the sound deep and pained, and

for a moment it looks like he's going to ignore my safe word. His darkened eyes catch mine, the overwhelming lust in them making him appear inhuman—but then he draws in a deep breath and begins to untie my left leg.

For a moment I'm stunned silent. Then I whisper, "Thank you."

"We had an agreement." His voice is a low growl, raising goosebumps along my skin and tightening my nipples. Thick fingers brush against my thighs as they deftly undo the final knot to allow me to stretch out my left leg. "If you want to give up two hundred and fifty grand, that's your choice to make." He reached for the silky ribbon tying my right leg.

A small twinge of regret at the reminder of the insane amount of money I'm giving up makes its way through my fear, but another glance at his insane dick makes the horror return full-force. "I-I'm sorry, but that's... you're too big. I can't. It won't fit, and you'd break me—"

He scoffs. "That's what you said about the toy you just took. You're female, Eve—you were born to open your pelvis." He leans in over me, his eyes intense as he holds my gaze. "And I know how to open you, baby girl. I've never *broken* a woman—and I never will. Especially not you."

There's sincerity in his eyes past the still-over-whelming lust making my core weep with longing. *God, he smells good. Why does he smell so fucking good?*

Two hundred and fifty-seven thousand dollars...

I eye his humongous cock again. "H-how would you... How would you not break me?"

The alpha's eyes turn hooded. He lets his fingers slide up my still-restrained right leg, all the way to my splayed pussy. He circles my drenched opening once, then draws his fingertips up to ghost them over my clit. I suck in a sharp breath at the zing of sensation.

"The female body is magnificent. The things it can do take my breath away... How it can move with such grace and strength, bring powerful men to their knees... Grant pleasures without equal... Give life." His fingers dip into my still-open sheath, gathering my cream before he returns to my clit with more insistence. Without meaning to, I groan.

"Such a beautiful, powerful thing needs to be worshipped... treated with respect. And that, Eve, is how I'll open you without causing damage. It'll hurt, but you were born to withstand pain. In your most primitive state, you might even enjoy the agony of opening your pelvis for a man big enough, strong enough to dominate your pussy into submission. But even as I make you gape and ache, even as I conquer you like no one ever has and no one ever will again, I will worship you like you were meant to be. I'll take you slowly at first. Teach your body how to open. Make sure you're wet and relaxed."

I can feel my pulse everywhere, throbbing in my

veins, in my temples, and especially in my abdomen. His words; his deep, rumbling voice; his fingers on my clit; the money; his overpowering scent filling my nostrils with rich musk and my body with a deep, all-consuming *need*...

"Okay," I rasp.

"You rescind your safe word?" His voice is almost a whisper, but laced with satisfaction.

I wet my lips. "Yes. I rescind it."

"Good," he says, and I get the sudden and over-whelming sense that I've been thoroughly manipulated. But before I can react to the disturbing thought, the alpha begins to rub my clit in firm, fast circles, and my focus scatters as pleasure rises sharply through my pelvis.

He stops before I can get there, pulls away, and chuckles as I whine.

"Let's get you tied back up before we continue, hmm?" he purrs.

"Why?" I protest, frustration at being denied an orgasm lacing my voice. "I've agreed to this—you don't have to restrain me."

He gives me a heated look as he pulls my left leg back up and out, easily wrapping the silky scarf around my ankle and thigh. "It's for your own safety, baby girl. You don't want to trigger me into putting you in your place, now do you? At least not until you've learned to take me."

The barely veiled threat shouldn't make my pussy pulse as hazy images fill my mind of what it'd be like if I fought back, if I triggered the latent alpha aggression already rough in his voice—but it does.

"Good girl," he purrs, clearly excited at the proof of my body's mutiny. With one big hand, he cups my traitorous sex. "I knew you were special. You'll learn to like it before we're done."

I want to deny it, but every cell in my body throbs in agreement.

God, I'm such a fucking headcase. I'm doing this for the money. *Just* the money!

The intruder ties the final knot in the red ribbon around my thigh, leaving me open and vulnerable. And then, finally, he settles his huge body on top of mine. His monstrous cock slaps up against my pussy, already looking for the way inside on instinct alone, and my lusty thoughts freeze with renewed fear at the meaty contact. Shit, he feels even thicker than he looks!

The warmth of his skin and the scent of alpha overwhelms my senses, but it's not enough to quell the terror making me whimper at the silky, iron touch of him. I suck in a panicked breath, gritting my teeth to stop myself from frantically babbling "mistletoe" again.

"You'll be okay. I promise," the intruder grunts. He sounds pained—as if holding back for as long as he has is physically hurting him. Keeping most of his weight on one elbow so he doesn't squash me, he reaches out for the drawer with his free hand, pulling out a bottle of lube he must have brought with him.

He pumps an obscene amount onto his palm, then reaches between us. Slick sounds and his arm's movements tells me he's smearing the full length of his cock in the viscous substance, but I don't see how it'll make any difference—I'm already embarrassingly wet.

Gritting his teeth, the alpha guides his member to my still-opened hole.

The sensation of his hot, wet cockhead pressing against my most intimate flesh is nothing like the dildo—and my body's reaction is entirely unexpected.

Apparently unaware of the horror it represents, the second his dick glides against my inner labia, my pussy melts, awakening instincts clearly not charged with my survival. Tendrils of excitement fire through my pelvis and into my blood, heating it, and I feel my opening *soften,* welcoming what lies ahead.

The alpha groans at the contact and buries his face in the crook of my neck. His breaths come in sharp pants, the sound of them in my ear drowning out the rest of the world until all I can sense is *him*—his weight forcing me into the mattress; the warmth of his skin everywhere we're pressed together; the raw scent of alpha in my nostrils; and his hot, slick tip nudging at my weeping entrance.

"I can't," I whimper, even as my pussy yawns eagerly for penetration. "I can't!"

"Shh, you'll be okay," he rumbles again, the barest note of compassion making its way through his dark lust. " Just breathe, gorgeous. I'll go slow."

Just breathe? Is he insane? Fucking Lamaze isn't going to stop my pelvis from breaking if he shoves that ridiculous cock inside of me!

Panic spears through my brain as my pussy lips part for his obscene girth. "I can't do this! Mistl—"

He silences me with a deep kiss. His lips are scorching on mine, his tongue plundering my mouth. Dark pleasure drowns out my panic, endorphins flooding my brain as I lose myself to the deep, commanding strokes of his tongue against mine. When he finally pulls back, we're both panting.

"You can take me," he promises huskily. "Your pussy was calling to me from the moment I first saw you. You were made to take me."

And with that, he puts weight behind that mammoth cock of his, forcing my labia wide.

The stretch is vast, and I hiss out a breath and claw feebly at air as my lower lips pull tight. There's an overwhelming sensation of pressure and *heat,* and then a sting of overextended flesh that quickly turns to a burn.

"Ow!"

"Shh. You're doing so well. Relax your pelvis." His voice is raw with restraint and unmistakable pleasure.

Slowly he puts more pressure behind his hips, and the burn turns unbearable.

"No!" I shriek, panic making me thrash uselessly to try to dislodge him—but much to my surprise, he eases off just a little. But before I can suck in a breath of relief, he pushes against my aching hole again, stretching my opening painfully as it desperately tries to take him in.

"No-*oh*-w!"

Again he eases off, then rocks his hips forward once more, over and over in an unrelenting rhythm, giving me a second's respite in between bouts of painful pressure. It's enough to make it bearable, enough to allow my body to take over again and attempt to obey his demand to relax my pelvis.

Slowly the burn of his attempted penetration softens to discomfort, and my whimpers lose some of the panicked edge.

"That's it," the intruder rasps against my ear. He strokes a hand between my breasts, over my stomach, and down to my mound. "You need this as badly as I do. I'll show you."

When he flicks a thumb over my exposed clit, I shudder at the raw sensation. But despite being so thoroughly wrung for orgasms from his previous ministrations, a shiver of pleasure runs through my little bud at his uninvited touch.

"Oh—*mmh*." I mewl at the confusing mix of sensations as he continues gently rubbing my clit while he rocks his cock against my stretched pussy. The zings of pleasure distract from my discomfort, and soon I feel the first stirring of another orgasm.

I don't know how he does it—how he tantalizes my overspent nerves and makes me yearn. I moan into his neck and rock my hips up for more, my focus slipping from the threat of penetration to the promise of pleasure.

It's exactly what he's been waiting for.

The moment I cant up against his thumb, he brings his hips down hard. Once again his cockhead catches in my opening, but this time instead of easing off, he uses our combined momentum—and shoves through my tight hole.

TEN

MISTLE...OOOH!

Blazing agony sears up my spine as my opening is forced much too wide. I shriek and thrash to dislodge him, but there's no saving my poor pussy now that he's finally breached me. Everything's heat and pressure—and a burning ring of fire.

"Take it out! Take it out!" I don't care that my screams have tipped way past the point of hysteria. All I care about, all I know, is that horrific sensation of being forced much, much too wide. *It hurts.* It hurts, it hurts, *"It hurts!"*

"Fuck," he groans against my ear, his voice nearly as tormented as mine, though not from pain. "Breathe. *Breathe.*"

I can't comprehend his words—I don't exist outside the world of sensation. I'm reduced to a writhing mass of flesh and firing nerve endings, so when he starts rubbing my clit again, but much more aggressively than before, I have no defense against the sudden onslaught of forced pleasure amidst the horror of being gaped.

"*Nonononooooo!*" My orgasm strikes like lightning, my muscles locking tight around the too-thick intrusion.

"*Shit.*" The alpha's grunt is pained, my pussy's iron grip on his sensitive head hurting him too, but I'm too far gone on my tortured climax to get any satisfaction from his pain.

Forced too wide to contract with the throbs of orgasm, my poor pussy flutters desperately as I sob and come in hard, painful spasms.

And still he rubs my clit, dragging my torment out with wave after wave of pleasure until I have no more left to give.

The relief when my muscles finally ease up and let me sag back into the mattress is blinding.

"That's it. Good girl. Just like that." His breath teases my earlobe, the roughness of his voice drawing goose-bumps up my spine. "Keep spreading that pussy, and you'll learn to like it soon enough."

I whimper wordlessly, too wrung-out to object. He's still in me, still gaping me hard on his awful girth, but the relief of no longer being forced to clamp down in orgasm makes it almost tolerable.

"I know, darling. It'll feel good soon." Strong fingers

move from my spent clit to my cheek, cupping it gently. "Breathe with me."

He inhales slowly, and I draw in a shaky breath, mimicking his rhythm on instinct. My nostrils fill with his scent, sharp animalic notes mixing with musk, and my core flutters in immediate response.

"*Ah!*" I squeeze my eyes shut, expecting pain, but when my pussy grips him this time, raw pleasure crackles up my spine instead.

"*Fuck,*" he groans, and when my eyes fly open in shocked disbelief that there is *pleasure* in this grotesque penetration, I'm caught in his heated gaze.

"Nothing, *nothing* has ever felt like you," he rasps. And then, with slow, firm pressure, he pushes home.

The thick bulge of his cockhead moves slowly through my reluctant pelvis, forcing me open all the way up in one long, agonizing slide. I howl, pleasure waning at the unbearable fire of his shaft spreading me so deeply, it feels like he's molding my body to fit his, shaping me until I am nothing but an extension of him—warm, trembling flesh made for him and him alone.

Every nerve in my taut sheath shrieks at the strain, and I'm sobbing for mercy in between hard gasps as he slowly, mercilessly sinks deeper—until finally, he's *there.*

The broad tip of his cock brushes gently against the bottom of my channel, the conquering of my body punctuated by a deep groan and the heavy slap of his balls against my ass.

"Eve." My name rumbles out of his chest with all the reverence of a prayer. Groaning again, he presses his lips to my ear. "I've never... I never thought... *fuck.*"

My only response is a whimper.

"I know, baby girl. Just breathe. Relax your pussy. This is what you were born to do."

Easy for him to say. I bare my teeth, wanting to snarl at him, but all that escapes me are hard gasps. I lie there, spread and vanquished so completely I feel him all the way into my bones.

But despite the impossible fit, despite how no woman should be able to enjoy this, somehow... somehow, I do. Through the cocktail of adrenaline and endorphins, I have the hazy thought that maybe he's right. Though my pussy aches from the strain and my pelvis is opened much too wide, I'm taking him. Completely. And it feels... It feels...

A low moan escapes my throat when deep tendrils of pleasure crawl up my thighs and sink through the screaming of angry nerves. *Oh, god.* It feels *good.*

"That's it. Good girl." His warm lips brush my jawline, then my mouth, followed by his large hand briefly cupping my breast. He rests his forehead against mine, groaning softly. "God... You're not supposed to feel like this." He pulls back to look down at me, and there's shock and awe in his lust-hazy eyes.

I'm too wrapped up in the physical sensations of his grueling penetration to care. My entire world consists of hot, stretched flesh and the sick, instinctive knowledge that my one purpose in life is to accept this alpha into the depth of my very being. He's right—this is what I was made for.

For him.

Then he moves. Everything turns white.

I think I'm screaming. I'm not sure. Liquid fire burns through my pelvis, hot and *wet*. My bones flex, my flesh squelches, and every nerve in my pussy lights up until I can't think, can't *breathe*.

"M-mis... Mistl... Mistle...!"

His thumb returns to my clit, massaging in time to the agonizingly slow rolls of his hips, and I *break*.

"Shit! Shit, no! No—*oohhhw!*"

My climax strikes through me, bright red ribbons slashing through my world of white nothingness. My pussy clamps down tight, forcing him to still his thrusts. I hear him groaning in pained pleasure through the roar of blood in my ears, faintly feel his strong fingers dig into my hips hard enough to bruise, but all my focus is on the pulse of orgasm wrenching me apart from the inside.

I come until every nerve in my body is screaming for

mercy, shaking my head in denial as tears spill down my cheeks. It's too much, too much, I can't—!

The alpha lets out a strangled, *"Fuck!"*, one hand releasing my hip to cup my cheek, pulling me into his neck. He withdraws halfway, growling, and then reaches between us with his other hand. Hot, wet spurts of semen coat my fluttering cervix.

My climax fades slowly, leaving behind a warm haze of utter physical and emotional exhaustion underlined by a deep ache where he still fills me so completely.

I blink up blearily at the masked man as he pulls back onto his knees—and then croak in utter shock when my gaze falls to where we're still joined. He's got one large hand wrapped firmly around the bottom of his cock, where his knot—oh my fucking god, his *knot*—balloons obscenely, forcing his fingers apart.

If I thought his dick was absurd, it's nothing compared to the absolute horror of his knot. It's so huge that even this oversized alpha can't fully contain it in his fist.

A heady cocktail of relief and gratitude floods through me when I realize he made sure to knot outside my body. If he'd forced that ridiculous thing inside me, I would have ripped in two.

The intruder senses my eyes on him and looks up from our joining, catching my gaze in his.

"Eve," he murmurs, his eyes softening. He releases his knot and slowly, carefully pulls out of me.

I groan as my pussy reluctantly releases him, my flesh swollen and tender. The relief when his wet cockhead finally pulls free is nearly as blissful as the orgasm he forced from me.

"Shh, my precious girl," he murmurs, gently caressing my cheek. His thumb strokes over my cheekbone as he looks down at me with a tender, yet possessive expression in his unsettling eyes. "You did so well. Just breathe for me."

I obey on instinct, my body light on endorphins despite the heavy throb between my thighs. Air fills my lungs, and I let out a raspy sigh.

The alpha frowns down at me and gets to his feet. Without a word, he leaves my bedroom.

"W-wait," I call after him. Is he leaving? I pull on my bindings, desperation trying to make its way through the hormonal fog of bliss. "Wait, don't go!" I'm still trussed up like a turkey—if he leaves me like this, I'll—

The wooden floorboards creak under the alpha's heavy weight as he returns to my bedroom, a glass of water in his hand. He sits down on the bed by my side and gently lifts my head, holding it up as he tips the glass to my lips.

"You think I'd leave you bound and helpless?" he asks, a dark note to his voice.

I'm too busy gulping down water to answer—not that I know what I'd say. After what he just did to me, I don't know what else he's capable of. The way he wrenched my body open felt violent, even though he was achingly gentle. And the way he looks at me now, with that deep possessiveness flaming in his eyes as he tends to me...

A shiver runs down my spine.

"You're still scared of me," he says softly. He puts the glass on my bedside table and cups my cheek again, tilting my head so he can look into my eyes. "Perhaps you should be. I've never felt like this with a woman before. I'm not sure what I'm gonna do with you, Eve, but abandon you? Helpless? Never gonna happen."

"Okay," I whisper, because what else am I supposed to say? He looks at me with utter sincerity, but there is something darker in his eyes too. Something that makes the most primitive, most female parts of my brain shiver with unspoken recognition. He might not have put words to the unsettling urges roiling inside him yet, but when he does...

I've heard the stories. We all have. Of women getting dragged into a dark alley, taken by an alpha in rut... and then claimed. Forced into a lifetime of submission.

As I stare up at the intruder, at the possessive glint in his eyes as he strokes my cheek, I fear I will share their fate before the night's over.

"So frightened, baby girl," the alpha murmurs, his nostrils flaring as he takes in my scent. "Haven't I proven

I'll be good to you yet? Perhaps you need a little more convincing..."

He leans down and presses his lips to mine, and my breath hitches at the soft velvet of his kiss. Warmth floods my body and soothes my mind, and I moan into his mouth despite myself.

"You make me ache, Eve," he rasps against my lips. He trails kisses down my jawline and up to my earlobe, biting it gently. "I fear I'll never get my fill of you."

"Please. You had me already. Just let me go," I plead, even if my voice is too raspy, too needy from his sinful lips to sound convincing. "W-we had a deal."

"The deal, my sweet girl, was for the night." He pulls back, towering above me as his hand slides down between my thighs, cupping my unprotected pussy. "And we're just getting started."

ELEVEN

STOCKING STUFFER

Thick fingers slip between my labia and immediately find my swollen clit. I moan, half in protest and half from pleasure, because despite how thoroughly overstimulated I am, his touch still feels so good. Like every molecule in my flesh is attuned to his.

"There's a good girl," he purrs, dipping his fingertips in the pool of our mixed fluids dripping onto the mattress between my thighs before he gently pulls back the hood of my clit, fully exposing the tender pearl beneath. "I love the sounds of your pleasure, baby girl. Your grunts and moans—so raw and animalistic, and just for me."

"Shit!" I spit when he puts his index finger directly on the tip of my clit. Sharp zings of sensation shoot through the little bud and deep into my aching pelvis. My worn muscles tremble, and I bite my lip to keep from crying out from the discomfort of my overstretched flesh contracting.

"Shh, breathe through the pain."

I pant and strain against the bindings keeping me tied down and spread open, hissing another curse as my clit throbs under his finger. But the ribbons don't relent, and neither does the alpha. Undisturbed by my cursing, he continues to rub firm little circles into my trembling nub of nerves, and there is nothing I can do but take it.

"Breathe, Eve," he says again—a dark command.

Shakily, I obey. Air laden with alpha pheromones and the smell of sex fills my nostrils and sinks into my lungs. Again I breathe, deeper this time, and again.

"Good girl, very good," he purrs, and so help me, the rumbly sound of his praise goes straight to my ovaries. Slowly the pain of my overworked muscles fades, and pleasure takes its place.

"God," I murmur thickly, rolling my hips up against his hand on instinct rather than as a conscious choice. *"Ooh."*

The intruder smirks at me, my moans of pleasure drawing him down on top of me again. His hips press down between my forcefully spread legs, the weight of him settling in the cradle of my thighs. "That's it. Fuck, look at you, cunt swollen and stretched and full of cum, and you're ready for more. I knew you'd be perfect, baby girl. Before we're done, you'll be begging for my knot. And

I'll give it to you, darling. I'll pump you full of cum and plug you nice and tight. Breed that pretty little pussy good."

Through the haze of my hijacked biology and the adrenaline as I feel his thick cockhead nudge at my splayed labia, the words *"knot"* and *"breed"* sink in.

"Wait... wait, what? No, I—*oooh! Shit!*" My panicked protest dies on a cry as the alpha rolls his hips and his cock pushes through my opening, spreading my tender flesh wide. He sinks in deep in one long, smooth slide, all the way to the hilt.

"Fuck!" His grunt of pleasure is underlined by my whine, because *goddamn*, he's still impossibly big, and my pussy protests the hard stretch.

I hear myself gasping "stop" and "no," but my voice comes from far away—from another woman refusing to say "mistletoe" despite her desperation as that brutal cock slides home. And I? All I can consciously process is the huge male on top of me, inside me, and that dark, agonizing pleasure of taking him completely.

The intruder moans brokenly, his hips, flush with mine, stilling with a tremble as he drops his head to the mattress. His soft lips brush against my earlobe. "You feel like life itself, Eve. Like this is my one true purpose— being inside you. You're all I need, darling. This is all that matters."

I barely have time to process his fevered words,

because in the next moment, he rolls his hips. Every nerve in my sheath flares to renewed life, and I cry out an instinctive protest, limbs straining against my bindings—but instead of pain, deep, wet ecstasy rocks through my body.

I gasp for air, eyes wide as the alpha pushes deep again, filling me. It feels... It feels *so good*. There is still discomfort as my flesh stretches to encompass him, but mostly... mostly there is pleasure.

Like life itself, he called the sensation of our joining.

He's right. That's exactly what this feels like.

I toss my head back into the pillow, relinquishing the panicked voice at the back of my mind frantically telling me this isn't *life*—it's danger, it's surrender, it's *wrong*. I don't have the capacity left to care. Endorphins flood my brain, and I moan wantonly as the masked intruder takes stroke after stroke in my wet depths. Right now, in these moments, this is my purpose—to spread my pussy and take him to the hilt until he has nothing left to give.

"Fuck yes, that's it, baby girl," he pants in my ear as my body softens in acceptance. "I'm never gonna get enough of you. God, you're so fucking addictive. I should have known the first time I smelled you... *Fuck!*"

He pulls back up, supporting his weight on his hands, eyes closing in ecstasy as he increases his pace. Sharp, rhythmic *thwacks* of his skin against mine underline my whimpering moans and his panting breath.

I don't know how long he takes me like that, deep and smooth and unrelenting. It feels like forever, yet only minutes before the rhythm of his harsh thrusts forces my exhausted body to climb.

"Shit!" I clutch my hands uselessly when my muscles tighten in preparation, and the pleasure immediately turns painful as my muscles grip his thick cock. "Shit, I'm gonna come!" It's a whine of dread, not delight, his presence inside me pulsing through my pussy and into my pelvic bones in hot, agonizing threads.

"That's it, baby girl, I've got you. Just let go," he groans, and despite the sliver of pain from my sheath's merciless grip on him, the rich, deep rumble of his voice is rough with pleasure. He pumps my pussy harder, forcing his cock through my pulsing tunnel mercilessly fast, drawing lewd, wet smacks from my depths as I howl in denial.

My protests are in vain. Despite the pain, there's no stopping the tidal wave rising through my abdomen and thighs. One minute I'm panting and frantic for escape—the next my entire body locks up in a tight bow against the ribbons tying me down.

"Holyshitgoddammitahhhh!" My cry of completion echoes through the room and nearly drowns out the alpha's growl as my pussy's tight spasms milks a release from him. This time, I feel the threat of his knot push hard against my trembling opening before he snarls a curse and

manages to pull back enough to clasp a hand around the swelling bulge.

"Fuck!" he spits through gritted teeth, his forehead pressing to mine as warm spurts of semen coats my cervix once more. He pants harshly through the expulsion, his orgasm sounding nearly as pained as mine, but he keeps his cock as deep as it'll go for the knot preventing him from going all the way inside.

Finally, some long moments later, my climax wanes. My muscles relax into one big, jellied puddle, and I sink deep into the mattress with a breathless groan. Everything is warmth and bliss.

Soft lips skim over my jaw, then press gently to my mouth. I sigh into the kiss, parting my lips willingly. For one long, euphoric moment, there is only pleasure, and a deep connection to this man who has shown me what it feels like to surrender everything I am to instincts I didn't know I possessed.

"You okay?" he murmurs.

Too shattered from orgasm to feel anything but floating haziness and a dull throb where we're still connected, I croak a weak, "I... I think so."

He kisses me again, then lifts his body off mine and gently pulls out. Semen follows his retreat, trickling out of my opening to pool on the mattress.

"God, you're beautiful," he rumbles, stroking his

warm hands up my thighs and down my shins. "How are the restraints? Any cramps?"

"No," I murmur, eyelids fluttering shut when he digs his thumbs into my hamstrings, massaging the deeper tissues.

"Good." He keeps massaging my thighs and calf muscles, and I allow myself to sink into the bliss of his care. This feels almost as good as the come he forced from me—and so much gentler—the warmth of his hands against my skin as comforting as a cashmere blanket on a cold winter night.

Once he's ensured my legs and hips are fully relaxed, he moves onto my wrists, checking the tension in the silk scarves to ensure my circulation is still good. His fingers brush against my palms as he does, and the intimacy of the gesture touches something deep in my chest. I look up at him and capture his gaze with mine.

"Why did you do this?" I ask softly. "Break into my home with the intent to force me? You're... gentle. I thought alphas were all about violence and power, but you're not. Not really. You could have just... asked me on a date."

He chuffs a breath, amusement flirting with the hoarse sound. "A date? Eve, it was all I could fucking do not to drag you into the alley by the station, clap a hand over your mouth, and have you against the wall in the freezing cold.

I'd love to have wined and dined you, baby girl, but the risk of you telling me 'no' at the end of the night when you saw my cock? Wasn't an option. But that doesn't mean I wanted to hurt you, not even before I realized... Before it became clear you crying with terror wasn't going to work, either."

Part of me wants to claim I wouldn't have told him no, but that part is currently drowning in pleasure hormones and not at all grounded in reality. Had this been a date, without a financial incentive and ample amounts of purring manipulation? Yeah, I'd have turned tail and ran the second I caught sight of his absurd dick.

"All right. Fair enough," I mutter.

The intruder's lips twist in an amused smirk, but instead of responding, he pushes off the bed, grabs my empty water glass, and disappears into the bathroom for a moment. When he returns, the glass is full again. He perches by my side and once more carefully supports my head as he tips the glass to my lips, allowing me to drink.

Once I've slaked my thirst, he lets my head sink back into the pillow. His dark eyes meet mine, and a tremor works its way up my body at the heat in them. He's still not sated.

My pussy aches as it contracts weakly in response to the need in that dark gaze, and I know I should plead for mercy.

I don't.

My nostrils are filled with his heady scent, and when he trails his warm fingers down my stomach and brushes them through my matted pubic hair before ghosting them over my protruding clit, my body comes alive under his touch.

"My God, Eve," he whispers, those blazing eyes roaming up my body. He doesn't finish the sentence, but he doesn't have to. The worship in his eyes as he takes in my sweaty, spent form is plain as day, even in the flickering candlelight filling my bedroom.

I've never felt this treasured, this cared for. I know it's

fucked up, and I don't care. When he lays down on his stomach between my forcefully spread thighs and runs his thumbs up each side of my labia, it's anticipation rather than dread that makes me gasp out a shaky breath.

"You smell like life," he groans, drawing in a deep breath. "The scent of us combined..." He presses his warm lips against my pussy, followed by his wet tongue. He licks down the open seam of me, and then flicks the tip of his tongue into my entrance, slowly swirling it around. The groan he makes when he tastes his own seed inside me makes my nipples harden and my clit pulse.

Pulling back long enough to slip two fingers up, he pumps them a couple of times, then hooks them, making me mewl when he rubs over my G-spot. But instead of continuing the stimulation, he pulls his fingers out and reaches up to my mouth.

"Open."

My eyes widen as I see the mix of semen and my own juices covering his digits. I don't get a chance to even think about protesting before he smears the white fluids over my lips. My tongue darts out to wipe it away on instinct, and the alpha shoves his fingers into my mouth. Salty, musky flavor explodes on my tastebuds.

"Suck," he growls—an alpha command.

I obey without thought, my tongue swirling around his fingers. The taste of us fills my senses, dirty and heady and completely addictive. I moan as something dark and base takes over my brain, and I form a tight seal and suck deeply, desperate for more.

"Good girl. Just like that. Keep sucking, baby girl. Know the taste of us." He keeps his fingers in my mouth as his own lips return to my opening. Filthy, wet sounds fill the room as he licks up inside me, feasting on my pussy and our combined spend.

I moan with every swipe of his tongue, and when he's finally finished licking every drop, he moves to my clit. My moans turn sharp, needy.

"That's it, let me know how much you want me," he growls against my molten flesh, then pulls his fingers from my mouth to thrust them back up inside my pussy.

I cry out as he flicks his tongue over my bundle of nerves, then sucks it deep into his mouth in hard, full pulls. It doesn't take long before I'm on the edge, and he doesn't relent. The deep, wet, pulsing vacuum he creates pushes me over, forcing worn muscles to contract as I come for his skillful mouth.

"Oh my God," I pant as he mercifully releases my clit and pulls away, letting me come down without overstimulating my trembling pearl. I look up at him, my eyes hooded from pleasure and exhaustion, and see the now achingly familiar need flame in his eyes. This time, when he falls on top of me, I lift my pelvis as much as I can despite my bindings, inviting him in.

"Thank you." His voice is a hoarse rasp in my ear, the

gratitude in it nearly drowned out by the gravel of primal urgency. Nearly. Our eyes connect for a brief, breathless moment, and in his dark gaze I see the relief of finally being wanted. He's never experienced that before, this powerful alpha who is used to taking what he wants. In this intimate space, in this single second, he allows the walls to drop, and I see the raw, vulnerable truth: he takes because no one has ever offered him anything, least of all intimacy.

Then he buries his face in my neck and presses his cockhead to my drenched opening, and my moment's clarity drowns in heat and the delicious ache of penetration.

"*Ah,*" I mewl, tensing up as he slides all the way in in one smooth push. But even as my exhausted pussy protests the stretch, it's not painful anymore. Not really. My taut flesh sends pangs through my nerve endings, but it's not agony this time. My pelvis opens around him, allowing him all the way to my cervix, and it feels like every molecule in my body comes alive.

"God, yes!" I moan.

He lifts his head from my neck and looks down at me, dark, needy eyes swirling with emotion I'm too full to comprehend.

"Eve," he rasps, and then he kisses me like I've never been kissed before. His soft, full lips dance over mine, not gentle but exquisitely slow, as if he's memorizing the feeling. He moans softly, tongue flicking in between my lips. He doesn't search for permission, but he invades my mouth gently, his tongue teasing at mine before it plunges deep.

He's still exploring my mouth when he begins to thrust.

I groan, but he swallows the sound, moaning in response as my pussy clings to his girth. A few more pumps of his hips and he breaks our kiss to let us both gasp at the shock of sensation. *God,* how does this feel so good? He's so incredibly *thick,* and I still remember the agony of that first penetration only an hour ago. But now? Nothing has ever felt this fucking amazing.

"More," I groan, half-delirious with the overwhelming pleasure he's fucking into me with each pump of his hips. He hits every single sensitive spot in my core, the rim of his fat cockhead mercilessly massaging my G-spot for every thrust until I see nothing but stars. "God, *more!"*

The alpha lets out a low growl, dominance flaming in his eyes in response to my demand. "You want more, baby girl? You want your greedy little cunt fucked hard, is that it?"

"God, yes!" I mewl, his filthy words doing nothing to slake the burn of lust pulsing through my clearly depraved brain and wanton body.

"Then that's what you'll get," he growls. Without

warning, he lifts onto his hands for leverage and snaps his hips down hard, forcing his cock deep in one, rough push.

"Shit!" I cry out, then gasp brokenly as that first blow is immediately followed by another, and another.

"That's it, take it just like that," the alpha grunts, each word punctuated by wet smacks of my pussy opening wide for his cock. "I'm gonna pump you full of cum, knot you hard. Put a baby in you. *Fuck!* Make you mine."

On some faraway plane, I know his words are terrifying, but I'm too lost to the dark pleasure of being taken so completely I no longer feel like an independent organism. As I lay tied down and spread open, I become nothing more than an extension of him—a receptacle for his desperation, his need.

In this moment, my only purpose, my only use, is to take him and everything he has to give me.

"Deeper!" I plead, mind gone on the burn of ecstasy and some wild, primal urge I don't understand rising from the darkest parts of me. "Please, I need you deeper!"

"I'll be in you so deep you'll never be alone again," he pants as he keeps fucking me into the mattress. The rhythmic blows of his body against mine send ripples of pain through my hip bones, but I'm too focused on the delicious feeling of his cock to care. "You'll carry me in your womb. You'll never forget who you belong to."

I belong to him.

The thought whispers through my mind and throbs in

my veins with the primal knowledge that he's right—I'll never forget I'm his; his alone.

I come so hard I see stars.

"God, your pussy kills me," he groans as my body grips him tight enough to momentarily still his thrusts. He moans brokenly with me as my orgasm makes my core flutter around him in hard spasms. The moment my muscles ease and I sink back into the bed in a blissful haze, he fucks me again. Harder. Faster.

"Wait, wait!" I plead, shifting in the ribbons tying me in place as my body is forced from the afterglow and back into a ruthless climb. "Please, just—oh! Fuck!"

The rest of my plea dies on a groan. There's no stopping this alpha; I've known that from the moment he grabbed me from the shadows and covered my mouth. My body obeys, overworked muscles forcing reluctant pleasure through my trembling nerve endings, and I pant underneath him, lost to the undertow of his all-consuming need.

"You're so beautiful when you submit. My perfect girl. I'm gonna knot you until you can't breathe without me. I'll show you exactly what it feels like to be mine."

Knot me?

My recent orgasm allows enough blood to my brain that dread makes its way through the pleasure haze of sex.

"Wait, you're not... God, wait—slow down! You're not gonna knot me, right?"

"Yeah, I'll knot you, baby girl," he growls, eyes flaming with possessiveness as he stares down at me, never easing up on his hard thrusts. "And it'll hurt so good, I promise."

Not exactly reassuring words.

"No, you can't, it's too thick!" I plead. "Please, please don't, you'll rip me apart, I—*oh! God!*" My voice dies on a whine as he presses his thumb to my exposed clit and rubs it roughly. Every thought in my brain scatters, replaced by white, hot sensation too intense to distinguish between pleasure and pain. I scream. There is nothing but primitive need and the heavy man on top of me, fulfilling it.

I come three more times, and he fucks me through each one, manipulating my clit when I beg for a break until my protests turn to wanton moans once again.

I'm so out of it that it takes me a while to register when the ache in my core turns sharper, each thrust stretching my opening a little harder.

My eyes fly open, and I stare up at the intruder, his eyes half-closed with pleasure as he growls each time my pussy swallows the full length of his cock.

He's about to knot.

"Don't!" I wail. "No, no, mistleto—!"

My panicked cry breaks off when his thumb once again finds my clit with savage precision, but this time, there's no hiding the truth of our coupling—the inevitable conclusion to sex with an alpha.

I gasp when the pleasure of his thumb melds with the

agony of stretched flesh as the expanding bulb at the bottom of his cock pistons in and out, until finally, it catches in my sheath on a withdraw, trapping him inside.

The alpha snarls and slams his hips to mine one final time, forcing his knot through the tight part of my pelvis. My pubic bones ache as my pussy opens just barely enough to let the intrusion through. I scream and writhe, frantic to escape until he's finally *there,* nestled deep. My body clenches down hard, enveloping him in a tight embrace—and I see nothing but white.

Through a rushing sound pounding in my ears, I hear the alpha roar in release, curses flying from his lips before he buries his face in the pillow next to me, muffling his snarl. His arms wrap around me, holding me so impossibly close while hot, wet spurts of seed spray my cervix. I feel every twitch of his cock, every tremor of his body. But the pain is gone.

It takes me several moments to realize I'm climaxing. Only as I start to come down do the waves of pleasure register in my screaming nerves. I moan brokenly, shaking with each flutter of muscles too stretched to contract.

"That's it. Just like that. Let go, darling," the alpha rasps against my ear, his voice rough with pleasure. He's shaking too, as if the sensation of my pussy clasped on his knot is nearly too much to bear.

It feels like forever before my body releases me from orgasm. Slowly my vision clears as I float back from somewhere outside time and space. I'm immediately greeted by a dull throb between my legs as the ability to feel pain returns. I groan in protest, my tongue still not fully capable of forming words, and then grunt when the throbbing increases to a deep ache as my nerve endings slowly wake up from burnout.

"I know," the alpha whispers into my ear, rubbing his nose against my temple in a soothing gesture. "You're okay. I've got you, baby girl. Just breathe through the pain." His lips feather of my cheekbone. "My brave girl, taking your knotting so well."

I look up at him, my lips trembling at the sensation of being tied so irrevocably to this stranger. But right now, he doesn't feel like a stranger. He feels like... he feels like he belongs here, locked inside me, making me ache in the most intimate way.

He smiles down at me, and though there is gentleness in his expression, dark possession still burns in his eyes. Fluffy white flakes slowly fall around us, and for a dazed moment I think it's snow. Like he's some dark winter god here to claim my soul.

Claim.

The word reverberated through my entire being. My body still throbs with the afterglow, and his presence inside me is unyielding. I feel claimed in every way. But I'm... not. Despite the possessiveness rolling off the alpha in waves, despite the knot tying me to him, and his growled words of ownership while he fucked me, he didn't bite down on my neck and claim me in his rut. He... bit the pillow instead, shredding it.

I'm lucky. I know that. Some girls come out of an encounter with a strange alpha with a claiming mark on their neck and an eternal bond forged to a man they didn't pick. And once my brain comes back from whichever stratosphere it's currently vacationing in, I'll feel gratitude. I know I will.

My chest tightens, darkness flirting with the edges of my heart.

I can't think about what we just did. How much it hurts.

Why I like that it does.

THIRTEEN
IN A MANGER
HIM

A singular tear trickles down her temple, and though no fresh bond ties us together, I can feel her despair almost like a tangible force as my chest reverberates with the ache of inexplicable anguish mirrored in her forest-green eyes.

"Eve," I whisper, kissing her temple and tasting her sorrow. "Don't cry."

"I-It hurts," she sniffles, but we both know that's not why.

"I know," I say anyway, because challenging her will only mean delving into my own need to complete the connection every instinct in my body is screaming for. Instead, I reach between us and find her well-tended clit.

She sucks in a breath, squirming underneath me, but my knot quickly makes her still, brows locking up in a frown.

"Nngh!" It's a sound of protest, but her pussy obeys my demand. I groan as her slick muscles squeeze on my knot, the sensation coaxing another trickle of semen from my cock. Damn, she feels so fucking good.

"Good girl," I rasp, pressing my forehead to hers. My entire body thrums as I rub her to another climax, her orgasm hitting hard and swift despite my thumb moving much gentler on her overstimulated flesh than before.

"Ah! God!" She cries out underneath me, pussy fluttering around my cock, and I feel the ache in my jaw to bite down on her neck once more.

"Fuck," I whisper hoarsely into the shared air between us, clenching my teeth against the instinctive need for everything she is. This... this isn't what I came here for, but I should have known... The moment her scent hit my nostrils, my body came alive like I'd never known was possible.

One night was never going to be enough.

"Fuck," I whisper again, burying my face in her hair as she comes down from her orgasm, body trembling under mine.

My mate.

The word alone sends my heart racing and my mind spinning. I always knew I'd find her one day, sensed her in my gut, yet I didn't go looking. Didn't make it a priority. But she'd been here all along. Alone. Waiting for me.

Unexpected guilt makes me grit my teeth. She should

have been by my side all along, under my protection. What if something had happened to her while I was too *busy* to be her damn alpha?

A chill runs down my spine as the reality of my choices hit me like a ton of bricks. What if something *did?*

"Has anyone ever hurt you?" The growled question is out of my throat before I can stop myself.

She blinks up at me. "Uh... hurt me? What do you mean?"

"Has anyone hit you? Violated you? Threatened you?" I clarify, my mind kicking into overdrive with all the ways she could have been harmed without me there to protect her.

"What, like, ever?" she asks, confused. "I mean, I work customer service, threats are kind of part of life..."

My eyes narrow to slits. "At work? You face threats *at work?*"

"I... I don't understand what's happening right now," she says, voice small.

I'm scaring her. The thought of someone getting aggressive with my mate while she's trapped by her need to put food on the table has my body hot with rage, and I know she can smell it on me. The stench of angry alpha has a tendency to send betas and women scurrying for cover—I know because I've used it to my advantage more than once. But right now, knowing my female's scared of me only makes nausea rise in my throat.

"Shh, it's okay," I murmur, forcing my rage down as I take deep inhales of her scent to calm myself. "Don't worry about it, darling. Just relax. I've got you now."

I do.

I lift my head to look down at her, and a wave of possessiveness courses through my body as our eyes meet. Fuck, she's beautiful—soft and curvy, with plump lips still rosy and swollen from my hungry kisses. And she's *mine*.

Despite my attempt to calm her, Eve still looks up at me with concern etched on her lovely face, and a kernel of shame sparks deep in my gut.

Why didn't I ask her on a date, she'd asked. I should have. Now *this* will always be how she thinks of me—as an aggressor, paying her to get what I want. But it's too late for regrets. I'm just thankful I didn't snap and fuck her up against a brick wall in a dark alley, because I sure as shit wanted to every time I followed her home while I learned her schedule and habits.

I know of more than one alpha who got his mate exactly like that, and the resulting strain on the mating bond is not something I'd wish on my worst enemy.

No, I still have time to make this right. I didn't claim Eve tonight, much as every cell in my body aches to, because she deserves so much more than a forced bonding. When I mark her with my claim, she will know who her mate is, and how far I'm willing to go for her.

I cup her cheek and kiss her swollen lips. The roil of

emotions has softened my knot, and I shift my hips, gently pulling out of her battered depths.

"Ow!" she hisses as my exit aggravates her raw channel, and I cover her pussy with one hand to soothe the tender flesh with my warmth.

"I know," I murmur. "I'll get you something to take the edge off."

Once she's settled again, I untie the silk scarves around her legs and wrists, spending some time massaging her limbs to ease any lingering discomfort. She sighs at my touch, eyelids fluttering closed, and I can't hold back a soft smile.

Even with my face hidden behind a mask, even after I've fucked her raw and made her take my knot, there's still an instinctive part of her that feels safe enough to doze off in my presence.

"Not yet, baby girl," I murmur, squeezing her thigh before I get up. "I'll leave you to sleep in a minute."

I make my way to her small bathroom where I've stashed the items I brought in preparation for tonight. I quickly refill her water glass, shake out two painkillers from the small bottle, and reach for the Plan B.

But as my fingers graze the foil packet, a whisper of hesitation makes me pause.

I've always made sure to never leave a woman without first making her take emergency contraceptives. The risk of pregnancy complicates things.

But...

I drum my fingers against the sink as the primitive urge to impregnate my female washes over me again. The thought of her growing round with my child, of knowing a part of my very DNA might be implanting itself in her womb in this very second... It's enough to make me hard with excitement, despite how thoroughly sated her magic little pussy's left me.

If she were pregnant, she'd need my protection even more. And as she grew larger, she'd be so vulnerable. She'd depend on me. For everything.

She's going to be mine, one way or the other. But if she's reluctant... Carrying my baby, needing a provider... that should motivate her to accept my claim willingly.

I put the Plan B back in my bag, then rifle through her bathroom cabinet, finding a Vitamin B supplement with a pill roughly the same size and shape as Plan B.

I make a quick trip downstairs to the kitchen, then return to the bedroom. Eve's still on her back on the sheets, legs splayed open and eyes closed. When I place the towel-wrapped bag of frozen peas between her legs, she stirs with a murmur, eyelids flickering open.

"Just something for the swelling, darling," I say, brushing a sweaty strand of hair from her forehead as she looks up at me.

"Thank you," she murmurs sleepily.

"Let's get you some water and something for the pain

too, hmm?" I say as I slide my hand from her forehead down to her nape, supporting her head. I press the three little pills to her lips. "Open."

"What's that?" she asks, clearly hesitant about accepting pills from a stranger. I feel a surge of annoyance that she doesn't trust me implicitly yet, but tamp it down. She'll get there, once my claim is brandished on her neck and my conscience is welded into her heart. "Tylenol. And Plan B."

Her eyes flash up to mine, surprise in her drowsy gaze. No doubt she has some memory of my verbalized desire to impregnate her during our coupling.

"I said I'd take care of you," I say patiently. "Getting to a pharmacy on Christmas would be a challenge."

"You planned for everything," she says, shaking her head in mild disbelief. Then she parts her lips, allowing me to place the pills on her tongue.

"I did," I agree as I grab the water glass and tip it to help her swallow. *Everything but finding my mate.*

Once she's swallowed the pills, I gently guide her head back down on the pillow and grab her blankets to cover her naked body. I linger by the side of the bed for a moment, fighting back the urge to keep touching her. Everything inside me aches to stay, to watch over her, but it's not the right time. Not yet.

"I'll make sure the money's wired to you first thing on the 27th," I say.

"Hmm," she hums, eyes closing again as she snuggles into the blankets.

Giving her one last, lingering look, I turn to the door.

"Wait," she calls softly. When I look at her over my shoulder, her eyes are open again.

"Stay. Please," she whispers.

"Stay?" I echo with a frown.

"Just... for a little bit. Until I fall asleep." She blushes, clearly as surprised as I am at her plea. But I understand why she's asking, even if she doesn't.

Women don't *know* the same way an alpha does when they meet their mate, but their biology will recognize him on an instinctive level. Eve doesn't yet know me as anything but the man who broke into her home and coerced her into spreading her thighs, but her body does. And right now, vulnerable and sore and high on hormones, she needs me.

"Okay," I say softly. "Until you fall asleep."

I return to the bed, my senses alight with the smell of our sex as I slip under the blankets behind her. She presses her back to my chest with a contented sigh. Her ass nestles in against my pelvis, and my cock immediately responds.

She stiffens against me.

I chuckle and wrap my arms around her waist. "Relax, baby girl. You've earned your rest." I press a kiss behind her ear, the scent of her in my nostrils stirring a flood of possessiveness. She fits so perfectly in my arms and against my body, like every molecule of her was crafted for me and me alone.

I let a hand slip to her belly as she relaxes against me once more. She falls asleep, safe in my embrace while I gently caress her soft abdomen, imagining how beautiful she'll look swollen with my child and completely and utterly dependent on me in every way.

Mine for the rest of eternity.

The next time I wake up, I'm alone.

I squint blearily against the dim light filtering through my woolen curtains, half expecting my intruder to still be somewhere in my bedroom, waiting for me to wake up so he can have me all over again.

A confusing rush of heat floods my muscles at the thought of that. I whimper when my pussy attempts a weak clenching in response. *Ow! Ow-ow-holy-shit-ow!*

Yeah, there's no way I'm going to spend time pondering whether last night was just a dream, that's for sure.

I lie under the thick pile of blankets, trying to quiet my breathing so that I might hear him. But there's no sound of life, nor the sense of someone else being in the room with me like there was last night. When I strain my hearing to listen for movement downstairs, there is only silence.

I don't know why my heart drops at that. Strike that—I do know, but I *really* don't want to admit it, not even to myself. Who hopes their rapist stays around to celebrate Christmas morning?

The same girl who asked him to stay and snuggle. *Christ.*

I grimace at my pathetically spiraling thoughts and force my stupid brain to return to a state that's at least semi-functional. It's not my fault. I can't help that my entire system is still flooded with endorphins, or that my bedlinens smell like sweet-spicy musk and male. The sooner I get out of bed and away from everything that reminds me of him, the sooner I'll be able to think without my ovaries' mushy interference.

Only the bed isn't the only reminder he left behind.

My abdomen protests violently when I roll myself off the mattress, and when I make my legs take my weight and force myself upright, my knees nearly buckle.

Yep. That still hurts. No wonder women who get a choice in the matter don't sign up for a second ride on this particular carousel. Perhaps I'd still be able to move with some dignity if he'd had me just the once.

Though if he had, I wouldn't have learned how good sex can feel. Jesus Christ on a cracker.

I shuffle to the bathroom while pretending it doesn't

feel like I'm still straddling a fencepost and manage to stumble into the tub. As much as I want to collapse into the warm embrace of a bath, I opt for switching on the showerhead instead. If I sit down right now, I'm not getting out again before New Year.

His semen is everywhere. Crusting down my inner thighs, matting my pubic hair, and streaked across my belly. Smeared across my butt and all the way up my lower back. I don't remember him coming anywhere but deep inside, but perhaps this is just what happens when your guy overfills you, then keeps pumping. Pure physics.

Not "your guy," Eve. Get it together.

There is nothing dignified about how I have to lean against the cold tiles and carefully—*ow, so* carefully—spread my labia with two fingers, then aim the shower-head up to rinse out my poor vagina. And oh, ew, yeah, he definitely deposited *everything* inside of me. The water softens the cream that has, for lack of better wording, jellied up there, and I stare in faint disbelief at the rivers of white semen rolling down my thighs and puddling in the tub around the drain. I should probably be more grossed out, but honestly, all I can think about is how if he hadn't given me that Plan B, I'd absolutely, one hundred percent be pregnant right now. I don't care what biology says about ovulation—there's no way in hell any woman's womb could resist that amount of semen.

"What a merry Christmas present that would have

been," I mutter. I mean for it to come out snarky, but my heart gives an odd sort of spasm. *Wow.* I *really* need to burn through this oxytocin high, *stat*.

<hr>

I'M STILL beyond sore after the shower, but I pull on my plaid PJs and fluffy slippers with only a little difficulty. The warm water's soothed my exhausted body enough that I can manage the stairs, so long as I walk gingerly.

Caffeine. I need caffeine.

I'm not prepared for the waft of vanilla, cinnamon, and coffee that greets me the moment I step into my small kitchen.

I flick on the lights and blink in confusion at the tray of cookies on my butcher block. They definitely weren't there when I came home yesterday. A glance at my coffee machine reveals a warm pot waiting for me.

He... made me coffee before he left? And... went out to buy cookies? Where can you even get cookies Christmas morning?

I pick up one of the heart-shaped ones and squint at it in confusion. It's perfectly decorated with swirls of sugar glazing and dusted with cinnamon. It looks like it comes from a high-end bakery, perhaps even Le Gâteau. I've been drooling over their window display all through December, but I only ever treat myself to one of their cakes on my birthday, because holy wow, do they charge an arm and a leg for a bit of sugary perfection.

I bite into the heart and hum a note of pure bliss. Definitely Le Gâteau. It's so damn good I don't even care if other adults don't have sugar first-thing. It's Christmas, and honestly, if there was ever a day I'd earned cookies for breakfast, it's today.

I shuffle over to my coffee machine and notice a small blister pack next to a note. A closer look reveals it's penicillin. The note is typed on thick, expensive paper.

If you are sensitive to urinary tract infections, have this with food and a glass of water. You will not need to worry about sexually transmitted diseases.

I stare at the note. It's *typed*. He's brought this from home. Just like he brought silk scarves so I wouldn't hurt myself while struggling, he's not only brought penicillin to prevent a sex-induced UTI, but also a prepared note with instructions on how to take it. I guess it goes with the Plan B.

I scoff in amused disbelief—probably not the sanest reaction, but oh well—and pour myself a mug of coffee. It's still warm, but it tastes like it was made hours ago.

I grimace and sip it anyway. How long have I been asleep?

A look at my microwave tells me it's nearly one p.m. I don't know what time he finally had enough and untied me, but I guess it's not that odd that I've slept in. I'm still worn to the marrow of my bones from the marathon ravaging.

I'm kinda relieved I opted for the sad Christmas Dinner for One microwave meal, or my holiday meal would consist of nothing but Le Gateau cookies. Not that that's the worst Christmas a girl can have...

I move to my fridge and open it to stare at the microwave dinner. An overwhelming sense of loneliness washes over me at the sight of the tin foiled sadness.

What the crap?

I wrap my arms around myself and push down the ridiculous *longing* that creeps up from the deepest recesses of my mind. *Nope.* Not going to so much as entertain that.

What in the world did you expect, Eve? Christmas dinner with the guy who broke into your home and paid you to fuck?

I close the fridge and return to the plate of cookies, intent on scarfing down at least three more with my coffee and forget about my hormones' insane influence on my brain, when a knock on my front door makes me jump.

FIFTEEN
STUFFED LITTLE TURKEY

Is it him?

I want to smack myself for the way my hearts speeds up at that thought. If it was, I should be *frightened,* not excitedly waddling to the door, coffee mug and cookie still in hand.

The frosted glass does not reveal a large, black-clad alpha. Instead I spy a woman around my own age, bundled up in a wooly scarf, hat, and mittens. She's carrying what looks to be several paper grocery bags in both hands and under each arm, squeezed tight to her body.

What in the world?

I quickly put the coffee down on my console table and unlock the door.

"Hey! Merry Christmas," she says the moment I open. "Where do you want this? The kitchen?"

"Hey, uh, I think you have the wrong address. What street are you after? Maybe I can help with directions"

She frowns a little and readjusts the bag under her right arm, though she doesn't lose her bright smile. "This is 220 Albert Street, right? Eve Compton?"

"Uh... yeah, that's me," I admit. "But I didn't order—"

"No, he said it was a surprise." She smiles even brighter at me and squeezes through my door, making me step back to make room for the filled-to-the-brim bags. "We usually don't take last-minute orders on Christmas morning, for obvious reasons, but with a tip that big... Normally I'd have brought someone with me to help carry and set up, but I'm having to squeeze your delivery in between jobs as-in. Really sorry about that. Kitchen's this way?"

"Yeah," I reply, mostly out of ingrained politeness, because my brain's taking its sweet time to catch up. "I'm sorry... *who* sent this?"

"Didn't leave a name—was adamant it remain a 'Christmas surprise.' Real demanding fella, but aren't they all?"

She barks a short laugh and elbows her way through to my kitchen, where she immediately starts unpacking the paper bags. Soon, my counter is covered in tinfoil trays of mashed potatoes, green beans, mac and cheese, cranberry sauce—made with real cranberries, from the looks of it—roasted and glazed carrots, a full-sized glossy-brown turkey, three whole pies—pecan, sweet potato, and cherry—tubs of gravy, bowls with stuffing, whipped cream and other assortments needed to dress a full Christmas dinner with all the trimmings.

It smells exactly like Christmas is supposed to, and I'm too busy salivating to care that I'll be eating turkey leftovers for weeks.

"Oh, my God."

"That's usually the reaction we get," the woman says with a grin. She pulls out a receipt and a pen from one pocket and hands it over. "Would you sign to confirm you've received your order, please?"

I do, still mostly stupefied at the sheer amount of food filling my tiny kitchen to the brim.

"Oh, and he asked me to pass on a message for you too." She pats her other pocket and fishes out a folded note. "He said, *'Tell her a woman who takes care of her alpha so thoroughly will never eat a microwave dinner again.'* So depending on how many alphas you've, ah, *taken care of* recently, it should narrow down the list of who's decided to treat you today."

She winks, probably to take the sting out of the most awkward message I've ever had relayed in my entire life, but there is no saving the flaming inferno rising in my cheeks.

"Oh, *God*."

"Don't worry about it; alphas are gonna alpha. But just, ya know, some friendly advice... If one of them's this possessive, might be a good idea to limit your dating pool. Friend of mine was seeing two alphas at the same time. One of 'em found out about the other, went straight to his workplace, put him in the hospital, then took a taxi to my friend's place.

"Next day she had a claim on her neck and a baby in her belly. She says she's happy now, but I'm not entirely sure she's not just high on the constant baby-making—five years in, five kids in tow, and a new career as a 'mommy blogger,' whatever that is. She was studying for the bar before he came along.

"Anyway, yeah, sorry, I know you didn't ask. Just... you seem a bit surprised that someone's taking care of you, so... heads up, I guess? If he's going hard on the surprises and presents, if you aren't careful, you might have a husband soon."

She thinks I take so many knots, I don't know which alpha is sending me surprise catering. Mortifying doesn't even begin to describe it.

"No, I... know who he is," I manage to choke out. "I just didn't realize he would..." My voice dies as I make a vague gesture toward the mountains of food.

"Ah. First alpha boyfriend, then? Well, at least he's got excellent taste in courting gifts. If you like the food, think of us next time you have a catered event." She slips me a business card and gives me a cheeky wink. "Perhaps a wedding, ha! Alright, I've gotta get back on the road. I've got eleven more drops before three. Happy Christmas, Miss Compton."

I'm still in a half-stupor when the woman—Noelle Hall from Hall Events & Catering, according to her business card—gets back in her car and takes off down the icy streets.

My first alpha boyfriend. I snort to myself as I close my front door to shuffle back into the kitchen. I guess that's a more PC explanation than *my first alpha rapist* paying me for my services in food.

I frown at the overflowing countertops. I don't like that word—not for him. It's probably still the oxytocin messing with my ability to think straight, but I don't feel raped. Ravaged, sure, and then some. But I also feel... cared-for. Treasured. No man's ever been so hyperfocused on my pleasure or my needs. And no one's gotten up and made me coffee before they split, nor ordered me a whole damn Christmas dinner as a thank-you for sex, that's for damn sure.

I know I agreed to the arrangement, but it was far more intense than I had any idea was even possible. Maybe I should hate him for making me experience such complete and painful submission, but I don't. I'm sure that means some part of me is broken, but right now, I don't care. It's Christmas, and I get to spend the day believing in magic and fairytales, and that I'm not fucked up beyond repair for wishing he was here, right now, to hold me and make me feel just as safe and protected as I did while I drifted off in his arms last night.

I pile a plate three layers deep, then cut a slice of each pie on a separate plate and spend a good forty minutes squeezing all the leftovers into my fridge and freezer. It's past two before I finally sink into my sofa, carefully balancing my tray, flick on the Christmas tree and reach for the TV remote. *Miracle on 34th Street, here I come.*

But before I can switch on my yearly cozy Christmas movie marathon, I catch a glimpse of something underneath the branches of my tree. It's a small parcel wrapped in snowflake wrapping paper.

What the...?

Gingerly I get back up from the sofa and waddle over to the tree to pick it up. It's light and tied with a silky blue ribbon. Underneath it someone's folded up a piece of cheap, blue-lined paper just like the notepad I have on my bookshelf.

Carefully, I unfold it.

My dearest Eve,

I didn't expect to find what I did with you. I

thought I just needed to get you out of my system, but that's not going to happen, is it, my sweet?

I brought you this token of my gratitude for the relief I was so certain I'd find between your thighs before I understood what you truly are to me. Now I know it's all wrong. Could I do it over, I would bring you a string of pink pearls as lustrous and full as your sucked clit, and woo you until you agreed to let me take you on that date you so richly deserve.

Nevertheless, the next time we meet, I will make my desires known far more honorably than I did this time.

I stare at the letter, mouth agape. It's a... I don't know *what* it is. My mind tries for love letter, but that's not it. It's more a declaration of intent. He's coming back for me.

I do my very best to ignore my aforementioned clit's heavy throbbing at the thought—and the subsequent twang of agony from my vagina—and shift my focus to the present.

Barring my middle school boyfriend—who gave me a sucker on a string the week before he broke up with me— no one's ever bought me jewelry before. Which I assume this is, given the size of the present.

I should probably be outraged that he thought he could break into my home, force me to have sex for hours and hours, and then buy me off with a pretty trinket, but honestly, I was thrilled with just the cookies.

"Highest of standards, Eve," I mutter as I tug on the ribbon.

Inside is a blue box. I bite my lip and open the lid—and nearly drop the damn thing on the floor.

It's a fucking *huge* diamond.

"That *cannot* be real." I lift it out of the box with shaking hands and realize it's attached to a thin gold chain. And *yup,* underneath it is a certificate of authenticity—the damn thing is real. *Real*-real. As in, I don't know the first thing about gemstones, but I'm pretty sure this little *thanks-for-pussy* present could easily pay for a luxury vacation to the Caribbean.

I stare at it for several minutes. Then I unclasp the chain, slip it around my neck, and sit back down on the sofa.

The diamond lies like a solid promise between my breasts as I dig into my well-earned Christmas dinner and flick on the first movie.

I'M through *Miracle on 34*[th] *Street* and halfway into *Home Alone* 2 when there's another knock on my door.

Frowning, I pause the movie and get up. Hopefully

it's not another food delivery, because I can barely move, as stuffed as I am from my surprise Christmas dinner.

But it's not Noelle from Hall Events & Catering on the other side of the door.

It's Adam McCain.

My boss.

SIXTEEN

SEASON OF ROMANCE

"I, uh. I'm so sorry," I blurt, because my brain immediately goes back to the last time I saw him—crammed in the executives' elevator and clinging to him for dear life—and all my panicked brain can think in that moment is that I'm going to get fired on Christmas.

"You're *sorry?*" he rumbles, eyebrows bunching into a confused frown as he shifts the bouquet of flowers in his arms—dark pink hellebores and deep red roses.

Wait... flowers? And... that voice!

I blink. *No.* That's... that's not...

But it is. And in hindsight, I should have known. How many alphas have I run into that have the money to pay a quarter of a million dollars for a one-night stand?

Or who smells so good my brain shuts down at his mere proximity?

"You're *him!*" I say, accusing—angry.

He sighs, his expression guarded. "Yes."

I gape at him, shock and a traitorous bloom of excitement warring in my gut. "You—!"

I have a million questions, but none of them come out as more than wordless sputtering. Eventually I give up and just stare at him. Adam McCain. Adam Mc-Goddamn-Cain. My boss. No, strike that—my boss' boss' boss' boss.

Silence stretches between us as I try to process how he went from looking like he wanted to fire me on the spot just from being in his Elevator of Privilege, to breaking into my home and making me feel things I didn't know were even possible... to now standing in my doorway. With *flowers*.

"Invite me in, baby girl," he says softly.

"Oh, you're asking now, are you? I didn't think permission was something that really concerned you all too much." My voice is tart, but I open the door wider and move to the side, because apparently the oxytocin high hasn't worn off yet and my stupid heart trembles at the naked plea in his eyes.

"Thank you." He steps over the threshold, his huge bulk taking up most of my small entryway, and closes the door behind us.

I look up at him, taking in the flakes of snow on his

wool coat, the gorgeous bouquet in his hands, and finally his sensuous lips drawn in a tight line, as well as the look of yearning in his dark eyes.

"What are you doing here?" I ask.

"I..." He lets out a huff and shoves the flowers into my arms. "I got you these."

I blink. "Um... thanks. But that doesn't answer my question."

Adam rubs the back of his neck, the plea in his eyes mixing with a look of uncertainty on his handsome features I'm certain no one's seen in a very, very long time, if ever. "Eve... Fuck." He sighs again and crosses his arms over his chest. "You know why I'm here."

"Uh, no. I don't," I say, frowning up at him from behind the huge bouquet. "Because if it was for more sex, I'm sure you'd have just broken in. Again."

"Damn it, woman, of course it's not for sex!" he growls. The sudden sound of alpha anger makes me take a step back, eyes widening.

My reaction makes his face fall, and he lifts both hands in a placating gesture. "Sorry, I didn't mean to... *Fuck!* This isn't how I wanted to..." He trails off and scrubs one hand over his face. "Eve, you're my mate."

I blink three times in a row. "Uh... I'm your... *what?*"

"My mate," he repeats, his eyes darkening with intensity as he looks at me, the uncertainty in his expression vanishing in a flash. As if saying that word out loud centers him. Hones him to a singular focus.

"I... that's... no," I stammer, eyes still wide. His *mate?* The implication roots me to the spot as Noelle the caterer's story about her friend who got forcefully mated flickers through my mind.

"Yes," he says, taking a step toward me and forcing his way into my private space. But instead of grabbing me, he gently cups my cheek. "And deep down, you know it too, darling. How you responded to me, how you needed me to hold you after... We are made for each other, baby girl. I'm your alpha, and you... you are my goddess. My reason for breathing."

"But I don't... I don't even know you," I protest. "And you don't know me. We can't be—"

"I know you," he interrupts me. "I know you bought this house when you could barely afford to. I know the pastry shop whose window display you like to look at, but never buy from. I know you walk a little faster when you pass a dark alleyway at night, and I know you browse gardening forums on your lunch break, even though you don't have a garden yourself.

"I've listened to you keep your composure when assholes scream at you on the phone for things that aren't your fault. I know your body. But most importantly, Eve, I know you're my mate. There's no arguing, there's no negotiating—you're the one."

I swallow thickly, a ridiculous rush of warmth flooding up through my chest and down my belly, mixing with the panic. The way he looks at me, so absolutely set in his belief, I know he's right—there's no arguing. He's made up his mind, and I can either get on board, or...

I draw in a shaky breath. "So... that's why you're here? To claim me, whether I want it or not?"

He lets out a rumbling noise and reaches for me. His fingertips skim over the diamond resting between my breasts. "You sound so reluctant. Yet you're wearing my gift—pretty jewelry instead of the necklace of semen you would be wearing if we lived in less... *civilized* times."

He flicks his eyes up to mine, capturing my gaze with his dark intensity once more. "You read the note. You knew I was coming back for you. And you put this on."

"Well, I..." I trail off, blushing as I'm forced to put words to my inner turmoil in the wake of my ravishment. "I thought... Maybe you'd, I dunno, court me. I'd never in a million years think you were planning on *mating* me."

Adam releases the necklace and lifts his strong fingers up to nudge at my chin. "I *am* going to court you, baby girl."

I blink up at him. "Uh... so you aren't...? You're not just going to... claim me and be done with it?"

He sighs softly. "I can see how you would have assumed so, based on last night. But no, Eve. You'll be my mate. You can't change that, neither of us can—but *when* that happens is up to you. I want you to *choose* me. So until you tell me you're ready, I will simply court you."

"Seriously?" I whisper, the memory of his dominance from last night refusing to let me fully trust in the absolute sincerity on his face. "What if I'll never be ready?"

His expression darkens and his hand tenses against my chin, and for a moment I want to slap myself. What if he changes his mind? What if he forces me—

But the darkness on his handsome features fades, replaced by a small smirk. "Oh, I think you're underestimating the lengths I'm prepared to go to to make you mine, baby girl. I can be very, *very* persuasive, and I *always* get what I want. Don't mistake my desire for a loving bond with leniency; I'm going to shower you with gifts and affection and orgasms until you get on your hands and knees and bare your pretty little neck for my claim."

"You think superficial things will make me love you?" I'm pretty proud of the haughty tone I manage, because the word "orgasms" has my sore pussy clenching with the memory of my sweet surrender last night.

He kisses me—soft and deep, his hand cradling the back of my head, making sure I can't pull away—not that I have the mind to try. His lips taste like sin and warmth and safety, and I moan despite myself.

When he pulls back, his eyes bore into mine. "You already love me; you just don't know it yet. But don't worry, darling, it's my job to make you accept the truth, and I won't rest until I have."

I don't respond. I simply stare up at him, at the alpha who's swept into my life, determined to change everything I thought I know about myself and the future I had ahead of me. Somewhere deep in the core of my being, the truth of his words echo faintly.

As if he sees the first reluctant seeds of acceptance in my eyes, Adam's expression softens. Gently he cups my face and kisses me again—light brushes of his lips against mine. When he pulls back, we're both breathing hard, and I'm halfway expecting him to carry me up the stairs, but to my surprise he asks, "Do you have any leftovers from dinner? I'm starving."

"Um, yeah. Loads. You *did* get me enough food to feed a small army," I say. Then, biting my lip, I add, "Thank you. For the food, and for the cookies. And the coffee. And just..."

Adam brushes his fingers over my cheek. "You don't have to thank me for taking care of you. It's my job now. And one I'm more than happy to do." Then he takes my hand in his and leads me to the kitchen, opening my fridge as if he already feels at home in my space.

I wrap my arms around myself as I watch him pull out trays of leftovers. It's... *odd*, seeing the mighty Adam McCain move around my modest kitchen. He looks so out of place in his expensive clothes, his huge frame taking up most of the room. And yet there's something undeniably comforting about it.

It's Christmas, and in the end, I'm not alone after all.

"Did you not have holiday plans? Family to visit, or some fancy rich person event?" I blurt.

"You asked me that in the elevator too," he hums, head still halfway inside my fridge.

"And?" I prod.

"And you're my mate." Adam reemerges with the final trays of leftovers, piles them next to the others on the crowded kitchen counter, rummages through my cupboards for the plates, and pulls one out. "Being without you is literally torture. I canceled what I could and wrapped up whatever obligations I couldn't as fast as possible, so I could return to you."

I raise both eyebrows as I watch him pile turkey and trimmings on the plate. "What if I hadn't let you in?"

Adam gives me a patient look before returning his focus to arranging green beans next to the piles of meat. "Then I would have spent the night outside, watching over you. And it would still have been a better Christmas than being at a *fancy rich person event* without you."

His words stir that stupid, soft thing in my chest I can't seem to get rid of when he's near. "Adam?" I ask softly.

"Yes, darling?"

"Did you... Were you looking for a mate? When we... met?"

"No." He takes the plate and lifts his chin toward the cupboards. "Grab us some wine, hmm?"

I obey on autopilot and follow him into my living room, where *Home Alone 2* is still paused and fairy lights twinkle around the window frame, as well as from within the branches of my neatly decorated tree.

"Then why—"

"Because as much as you don't get a choice, baby girl, neither do I," he interrupts me, turning that dark gaze of his on me with all the smoldering intensity of a predator. "It doesn't matter what either of us want. This is what Fate has decided, and we have no fucking choice but to obey. Understood?"

My wide-eyed expression makes his features soften. He sighs and puts down the plate on my coffee table, then turns to me and cups my cheek in his large, warm hand.

"No, Eve, I didn't plan to meet my mate that day in the elevator. But I did. And I'm not sorry it happened; I'm thankful, even if every second I'm not burying my teeth in your neck to claim you feels like having my fucking guts squeezed like a wrung-out washcloth. Being around you is like... like the world finally makes sense. Like I've finally found my purpose. And it's you, Eve. So please, let me take care of you. Eat with me."

My heart melts entirely in the wake of the alpha's

admission. I've never felt wanted before. Not truly. Not like this. And it's... overwhelming.

I close my eyes for a second, pushing back the prickle of tears, before I nod and place the two wine glasses next to the plates. "Okay," I whisper.

He settles into the sofa, his large frame making the rickety piece of furniture groan in protest, and lifts an arm in invitation.

I only hesitate for a second before I slip in next to him, allowing my still-sore body to press into his armpit where I fit so perfectly.

Adam wraps his arm around me with a soft sound and kisses the top of my head before he grabs the remote and hits play. Then he picks up his plate and, before taking a bite for himself, offers a forkful of meat dipped in sauce to me.

I accept it more out of reflex than any real hunger, but he makes a pleased sound at the back of his throat that warms me to my core. He truly does find purpose in the simple act of caring for me, however unfathomable that is.

Is this what love is supposed to be like?

I glance up at him and feel the first stirrings of something other than biological impulses as I watch him absorbed in the cozy Christmas movie.

Fate, he calls it. Inescapable. Unyielding.

Perhaps that doesn't have to be as terrifying as it sounds.

. . .

BY THE TIME the movie is over, I'm so full it'd be easier to roll than walk from the leftovers I've been handfed, including a large slice of pecan pie. Every inch of my body is warm and relaxed, and my head is comfortably resting against Adam's chest as he gently strokes my hair.

"How's your pussy?" he asks, his voice low and intimate.

I blink, some of my lethargy withering at his blunt question. "Er... still pretty sore. Please don't... I really don't want to..."

He chuckles, as if me pleading for mercy for my poor vagina is just too adorable. "Don't worry. We can watch another movie instead. Would you like that, baby girl?"

"Yes. Please," I quickly agree. I'd probably have agreed to watch a gory horror film to save myself, but I don't tell him that.

"All right, let's see what we've got here... Which one do you prefer, *The Christmas Chronicles* or *How the Grinch Stole Christmas?*"

"Either. I love them both."

He gives me a soft smile and nudges my chin with the crook of his finger. "My mate loves her Christmas movies. I will remember that."

"I love everything about the holidays," I say as he puts on *The Christmas Chronicles.* "The food, the decorations, the music, the festivities... There's just something magical about this time of year."

"I admit, I've never really considered this time particularly magical... but I think I may now. It will always be the season I met my mate."

"What do you mean you never found Christmas magical? You run a business that sells children's toys!" I protest, mildly outraged.

Adam chuckles and gives me a tight squeeze with the arm he's got around my shoulders. "You have a point. Perhaps once we have little ones of our own to buy toys for, I'll care about more than the profits that company pulls in..."

I give his arm a smack for good measure—a move that just makes another chuckle rumble through his chest. "That's horrible. Your PR team would die if they heard you talk like that. And absolutely *no* baby talk. We barely know each other."

"Mm," he agrees mildly, petting my hair before returning his focus to the movie.

I relax in his embrace, my thoughts flickering back to Noelle the caterer's friend.

My alpha may have forced his way into my home, but I know I'm lucky. He could have forced a bond and put a baby in my belly against my will, but that's not the kind of man he is. Despite his baby-making dirty talk when he had me, the fact that he gave me a morning-after pill means he values my autonomy—as much as an alpha can, anyway. He wants my trust. And, ultimately, my love.

As I cuddle in closer to him, warm and safe and content, I know in the depths of my heart that he's going to get what he wants in the end.

SEVENTEEN
GILDED ORNAMENTS

Being Adam McCain's mate-to-be isn't as low-key and relaxing as our Christmas night together would have suggested.

He spends the night, climbing uninvited into my bed as if he has every right, and I don't protest until his fingers slip down between my legs to stroke at my clit.

"You said I didn't have to," I plead, the deep ache from my core as my muscles respond to the thrill of pleasure making me clamp my thighs together.

"You don't," he murmurs, still petting my little pearl delicately until I reach down to grasp his wrist. He finally stills with a small sigh. "I just want to make you feel good, baby girl. I won't penetrate until your body is ready again."

"It still hurts. Everything down there is just... used up."

He gives me an indulgent smile and pulls me into his chest. "I think my mate has a bit of a dramatic streak, hmm? Used up? Darling, I'm never going to be done with that magical little pussy of yours. But I suppose it's Christmas—if you really don't want to come tonight, we can wait until the morning. Would you like that? To wake up to me worshipping your clit?"

I narrow my eyes at him, entirely aware of the manipulation—he's trying to make me say I want him to touch me in the morning if I don't want him to do it tonight. But my clit is already tightening with anticipation at the promise of being *worshipped,* and I'm much too sleepy and comfortable to put up a fight.

"Okay," I murmur, nuzzling into his bare chest. "Tomorrow. But no penetration, all right?"

"No penetration," he agrees softly, warm lips skimming over my scalp. "Yet." Then he begins to stroke my back slowly and rhythmically, pulling me deeper and deeper toward the blissful haze of unconsciousness.

As I drift off to sleep, I feel one of his large, warm hands find my lower abdomen and curve protectively around it.

ON THE TWENTY-SEVENTH OF DECEMBER, Adam takes me to the bank to pay off my mortgage. It's a surreal experience to sit in the back of his Bentley as his honest-to-God *driver* navigates Mattenburg's busy streets. It's not really clicked for me until then that I'm *dating* a billionaire. I don't know why it takes a fancy car and staff members to sink in, but I'm guessing it's because up until now, all dating-related activities have taken place in my very modest little townhouse, and Adam has a way of looking remarkably at home there.

"Are you my boyfriend?" I blurt.

He glances at me, one eyebrow raised. "I'm your alpha."

"Well, yes, but..." My cheeks flush a little at the clear displeasure in his voice, and I give him a sheepish smile. "If I were to describe you to normal people. Y'know, who don't break into their crush's window and rape her."

"I didn't *rape* you." Despite the softness in his voice, there's a warning tone to it.

I roll my eyes. "Well, no, not technically. But you were planning to. *Anyway*—back to my question. What... What *are* we? Mates-to-be just sounds... so ridiculous."

He stares at me for a long moment, a hint of possessiveness in his eyes. "But that's what we are, Eve—mates-to-be, until you are ready to love me. Then we will simply be mates."

"What, so we aren't getting married? I won't be your

wife?" I ask, surprising myself with the note of disappointment in my voice. My blush intensifies. *Ridiculous.* Two nights ago I was busy telling myself I was only allowing him inside me for the chance at a mortgage-free life, and now I'm... what, *upset* that I don't get to walk down the aisle in a pretty white dress? God, his stupid pheromones are really screwing with my head!

"Eve, look at me."

My head turns toward him without my conscious intent, and I bite my lip with frustration. He truly has infiltrated every part of my biology, and I'm hardwired to obey my alpha. Yeah, he isn't wrong. That's what he is, even if I refuse to admit it out loud yet.

He cups my cheek, the comfort of his large hand already familiar. "I will marry you in a heartbeat, and I will be proud to call you wife. But those things... For alphas, they are superfluous. The only thing I need is my mark on your neck and our bond anchored safely in my heart—the knowledge that you are mine completely, including in the eyes of the law. But I understand that things might be different for you, and so yes—you will be my wife." He sighs softly, resigned. "And I suppose until then, you can call me your boyfriend, if that makes you comfortable."

Comfortable is probably not the right word, I think as I look at the stern alpha CEO who has reluctantly agreed he's my *boyfriend*. I still can't hold back a smile. Yes, my poor vagina has had a thorough lesson in alpha dominance, but it's the small moments of conceding the complete control over me, over us, he so very easily could demand that makes my heart flutter traitorously.

His demand that we become mates is born from a biological imperative, but letting me call him my boyfriend when it clearly goes against his alpha instincts to accept such a beta term, and allowing me to decide when we have full penetrative sex again, despite his constant, and probably rather painful, erection shows me there's more to my intruder than brutish animal instincts.

I reach out on impulse and take his hand, my slim fingers wrapping around his thick digits looking almost comical with the size difference.

Adam makes a small noise at the back of his throat. When I look up and catch his gaze, the softness there makes my heart flutter.

"I already love you," he murmurs, voice thick. Without waiting for my response, he pulls me into his embrace, kisses the top of my head—and begins to purr.

"*Oh,*" I sigh, the immediate calm flooding through my chest easing the pang of anxiety at his words.

Love, I think as I snuggle in against him, burying my face in his expensive wool coat so I can inhale his delicious scent.

"Would you have taken the stairs that day we met in

the elevator, if you'd known the outcome then?" My voice is already drowsy from the soothing effect of his purr.

For a moment he doesn't respond, and I think he's going to ignore me. But then, softly, he says, "I might have, if I'd realized how profoundly you'd change my world. I was told as a young man that meeting your mate alters your priorities, but I never knew how completely until you ran out of that elevator and a part of me left with you."

He kisses the top of my head again. "I will do anything for you, Eve. I'll give my life for yours, my dignity and every cent I own to keep you by my side. If I'd known my life would no longer be my own, it might have been enough for me to flee like a coward before we met and my fate was sealed for the rest of eternity. But now? If I could do it over? No. Just the thought of a world without you... it's unthinkable. Unbearable. The only thing I would have changed about our meeting is that I would have kissed you under that mistletoe, then asked you out for dinner."

"I think I would have said yes," I say, eyelids closing halfway as he resumes the soothing purr.

"If you hadn't, I wouldn't have relented until you changed your mind," he whispers in my ear. "You're mine, Eve. All mine. Forever."

Some distant part of me knows I should be alarmed by this, but as I sit in his arms, his strength and protection encapsulating me and his rich purr rumbling through my body, all I feel is contentment.

Clearly pleased, Adam deepens his purr and covers my lower abdomen with a large hand. He keeps it there for the rest of the drive.

The next morning, I wake in my bed alone.

I frown into the darkness, momentarily confused by the lack of being wrapped up in warm arms corded with thick muscle. It apparently only took me two days to grow accustomed to not waking up alone.

Real pathetic, Eve.

I'm annoyed at myself for the unsettled feeling clenching at my gut at Adam's absence, because wow, did I not take myself for being the kind of girl who'll grow dependent on her boyfriend in *two damn days,* but here we are.

I push the irritation aside, climb out of bed and pad down the stairs in my PJs.

I find him pacing in my living room, his phone pressed to one ear and an irritated scowl on his face. The room is so small—and he's so huge—it only takes him three strides to cross from one end to the other.

"...I don't fucking care. Get a security team here in no more than ten fucking minutes, and then find the reporter responsible," he snarls.

"What's going on?" I ask, unease creeping up my spine as the scent of his anger hits my nostrils. *Ugh.* Angry alpha is *the* most unpleasant stench on the damn planet. It's not that he smells bad—I don't think I'd find his natural scent bad even after a hard session at the gym—but my biology is hardwired to cower and placate an aggressive alpha, and there's nothing I can do to stop my nervous system from firing off alarms.

Adam turns to me, phone still pressed to one ear. He takes one look at my anxious face, hangs up without another word to the person on the other end of the line, and strides back across the floor to pull me against his chest.

"It's nothing for you to worry about, darling," he rumbles, petting my messy hair. "I've got it under control."

"Okay, but like... what's gotten you this riled up?" I ask, fighting back against his hold to free my face from his cashmere sweater. "Why does a security team need to come here?"

Adam lets me pull back enough so I can meet his eyes, then strokes my chin with his knuckle. "It's just a precaution. Some sorry excuse for a reporter snapped a picture of us when we were walking out of the bank together yesterday and blasted it all over the internet."

I blink up at him. "Uh, what? Why would someone do that?"

The answer is obvious—because I'm dating a freakin' billionaire business mogul, even though I conveniently keep forgetting that when it's just the two of us—but I can't fully wrap my mind around why anyone would care who he's dating. Or why that means we suddenly need a security team.

"Because people have way too much time on their hands and way too little going on in their own lives," he growls. "I don't care when they spread my picture for the vultures to feed on, but my *mate*? Who knows what kind of psycho will see us together and decide you look vulnerable enough to take on?"

I very studiously avoid making any sort of comments about what kind of psycho already found me vulnerable enough that he broke into my home. He doesn't seem like he's in the mood for zingers.

"It'll be fine." I gently pat his chest, indicating I want to be released. He doesn't relent until I put more force behind my arms to push away, giving me an annoyed grumble as I step back. "Why don't I make us some coffee? Once we've had some breakfast, I'm sure it won't seem as stressful."

· · ·

I'M INCREDIBLY, shockingly wrong.

Adam's security team arrives while I'm busy frying eggs. He barks orders at them, and then there are boot-clad men stomping around my tiny house, checking windows and working obnoxiously loud power tools to install some sort of security system I'm not even consulted about.

I grumpily remind myself I'm dating an alpha, and that along with an overbearing nature, he's burdened with protective instincts that make a mama bear look chill.

I feed my overprotective alpha, but leveling out his blood sugar does little to ease his agitated state. After a few more rounds of pacing through my kitchen and living room, all the while casting irritable glances out the window at the three bodyguards stationed in front of my house, he turns to me.

"This isn't working, baby girl."

I raise both eyebrows in question. "What's not working?"

Adam rubs the back of his neck and rolls his shoulders, but the stress still wafts off him in waves. "Your house. It's cute, but it's not safe."

"I mean, those three dudes outside look like they know how to handle themselves," I point out.

"They do, or they wouldn't be on my security team," he grumbles, looking so miserable with stress that I cross the floor to hug him.

"Do you *really* think someone's gonna take down three trained bodyguards, *and* you, just to get their hands on me so they can blackmail you or something?" I ask. "I get you're high-profile, but this level of anxiety seems a bit much for the situation, babe."

He gives me a soft look, and I realize it's the first time I've called him by a pet name. I blush, a little embarrassed.

Adam cups my face. "Statistically, no. The risk is minimal. But it's there, and it's driving me absolutely insane. I can't get the thought of someone hurting you because of your association to me out of my head, and I..." He trails off, but the rest of the sentence rings loud and clear in his pained gaze. He's not used to having someone soft and squishable to protect.

"Loving you is like having my heart suddenly out in the open, unprotected instead of safe behind my ribs," he murmurs, tormented eyes searching mine for any hint of understanding. "I need to know you're protected, Eve. Always. Every second of every day."

"I am," I point out, the desperation in his voice keeping my annoyance at the newly installed security system and bodyguards outside my door at bay. The poor guy looks like he's about to have a nervous breakdown.

Adam shakes his head and grips my face a little tighter between his palms. "It's not enough. I need you to move in with me."

My eyebrows lift high on my forehead, and I manage

to sputter, *"What?!"* before he interrupts me.

"Just for a little while, until any public interest in you dies down. A couple of weeks... A month, tops. Please, my love. I need to know you're safe, and my apartment is much more secure than your house. And private."

The earnest plea in his eyes touches something soft in my chest, and my resistance slowly fades. Moving in together this soon is preposterous, no matter how much he claims we're mates and fated to be together. But if it's for a limited time, and it helps him get out of whatever alpha mind-spin he's currently in, then fine. I can even pretend it's a nice little romantic vacation. I'm sure his place is swankier than mine anyway.

"Okay. For a couple of weeks," I say, giving him a reassuring smile.

My alpha's face lightens into a relieved smile that makes him look years younger. "Thank you, darling. You won't regret it. I'll take such good care of you you'll never want to leave," he whispers before brushing his lips over mine, quelling the brief flutter of concern his words cause at the pit of my stomach.

ADAM'S "APARTMENT" is a massive penthouse. It takes up the entire top floor of one of the new, luxurious towers downtown, complete with a wraparound balcony.

I gasp in amazement at every turn as he gives me the tour, halfway stunned that something this beautiful even exists in Mattenburg. The place is obviously expensive, with rich wood and stone finishes, but where I'd expected ostentatious displays of wealth everywhere, Adam's taste is pleasantly pared down.

"What, no helicopter pad?" I tease as he takes me out onto the balcony. The view of the skyline is amazing; I can see all the way across the river from here.

He gives me an indulgent smile. "No. It would ruin the tranquility I go out here for. And besides, where would you garden, if I took up our outdoor space with a big, ugly machine?"

"*Our* outdoor space?" I ask, eyebrows raised. "I'm going home in two weeks—maybe don't decorate with me in mind."

Adam's expression remains gently amused. "Sure. But you'll be coming to visit often after that. And eventually, when we mate, this will be your home as well. Unless you'd rather live somewhere else? Perhaps a nice country estate outside the city? It'd give me a reason to get that helicopter you mentioned."

I blush at the mention of us mating. "Look, it's *way* too early to be discussing living arrangements. Let's just get to know each other, okay?"

He smiles sweetly and gently nudges my chin. "Sure, darling. Whatever you want. Your wish is my command."

HE LIVES BY THOSE WORDS.

Everything and anything I want, Adam somehow anticipates. Foot rubs, sweet words of affection, indulgent brunches, lunches, and dinners, the occasional walk in the nearby park or trip to museums and the theater, all interspersed with gifts of jewelry, clothes, and books. I have no idea how he guesses exactly what I would love every single time, but I'm too high on the romance of it all to care.

At night, he takes me to his bedroom and overwhelms my senses with pleasure. He doesn't ask me whether I'm ready for penetration, despite the need burning in his eyes as he makes me climax with his skilled fingers and mouth. Instead, once I'm sated and boneless in the sheets, he finds his own release with my soft thighs pressed around his mammoth cock.

I know what he's doing. He warned me how he would charm me into falling in love with him, and as much as the sane part of my brain is warning me of his tactics, I can't deny that it's working.

It's not so much the gifts and pampering—though I'm not gonna deny both are very nice perks—as it is his intensity.

I've never been the center of anyone's world before. My parents love me, but they were very much the kind of parents who didn't believe in overindulging their child with attention. Previous relationships always seemed a balancing act of not showing too much affection, lest the power dynamic got skewed.

Adam has no such reservations. He makes it clear, both in words and actions, that I am his main priority. When we're together, I feel the warm burn of his attention at all times. When he has to leave me to take care of his business, I receive multiple texts to check in on how my day's going.

He also fires me.

Which doesn't sound particularly romantic, I know, but my release from his company is accompanied by a monthly stipend of a *lot* more than what I was making as a customer service rep. It also includes a sizable pension and comes with legal documents ensuring I will receive my stipend for the rest of my life, regardless of my association with Adam. He's really gone out of his way to show me my financial stability won't be dependent on when, or even if, I decide to become his mate. In alpha terms, that's about as romantic as it gets.

I'm so swept up in the bliss of falling for my billionaire suitor I only realize my period is late as I hover over the ensuite toilet on the morning of January seventh, retching up every ounce of bile in my system.

I go through the motions of wondering if I ate something dodgy the night before, or perhaps I picked up a stomach bug on our latest trip to the theater. Then, almost subconsciously, I mentally calculate when I last had my period.

Shit.

Shit, shit, shit.

But *how?*

The only time I've had full, unprotected sex was when Adam broke into my house on Christmas Eve. And he gave me Plan B right after.

Are the damn things not 100% effective?

I rest my head in my hands as I try to swallow the remaining nausea. I guess no birth control method is.

Okay, no need to panic just yet. It could still just be a case of dodgy clams.

After several long, deep breaths, I manage to get it together enough to peel myself off the toilet. I swish around some mouthwash, splash fresh water on my face, get dressed, and head to the front door. Adam's working this morning, and as much as part of me would love not being alone with the gnawing panic in my stomach, it's probably for the best that I don't have his overprotective ass hovering over me right now. Sometimes a girl needs to melt down in private.

But as I open the front door to head out to the nearest pharmacy, I'm met by a big, burly bodyguard outside.

"Ma'am?" he asks. I don't miss how he takes a half-step, his body blocking my exit path.

"I need to go out," I say, tone sharp.

He doesn't move. "Sorry, ma'am, I have orders to keep you safe inside the apartment until Mr. McCain returns."

I blink. Several times. "Excuse me? You have orders to keep me *imprisoned?*"

Okay, so as far as prisons go, Adam's penthouse is pretty luxe, and I'm mostly using the term "imprisoned" to highlight the ridiculousness of this muscle-for-hire trying to keep a grown woman from leaving when she damn well pleases.

Unfortunately for me, the bodyguard's face remains entirely blank. "I'm sorry, ma'am. I can't disobey orders."

My mouth falls open in disbelief. He's serious. He's not going to let me out.

Scowling at my impromptu jailor, I reach for my phone to call Adam and either break up with him or just scream—I've not entirely decided which yet—when the memory of why I was trying to leave in the first place sets in.

My fingers falter, letting my phone drop back into my purse. I don't want to talk to him before I know if...

...if my life's about to change even more dramatically than it did Christmas Eve.

"I need something from the pharmacy. Before Adam —Mr. McCain—comes home." I say, crossing my arms over my chest. "And just FYI—keeping me here against my will is illegal."

"I have orders to ensure you get whatever you need," Mr. Bodyguard says, ignoring my thinly veiled threat of legal action. "If you tell me what it is, I'll send someone to fetch it."

I hesitate for a long moment, but my options are seemingly rather limited. Finally, I tell him, "I need a pregnancy test. And some salty crackers, while you're at it."

If the news that I might be carrying McCain Junior startles the bodyguard, he doesn't show it. "All right, I'll have that to you in twenty minutes. If there is nothing else you require, please step back inside, ma'am."

I give him a tight-lipped glare, forcefully holding myself back from thanking him, and return to my gilded cage.

No doubt the bodyguard's orders are a result of Adam's tightly wound alpha instincts needing to know I'm safe at all times. I'm still going to absolutely murder him when he returns.

Unless it turns out I'm pregnant.

Then I'm going to have a panic attack.

Possibly still murder him, but not sure how I'd explain to my baby that I killed its daddy.

My baby.

The thought settles heavily in my chest. I pause, my mind coming to an odd sort of stillness as my hand moves to my lower abdomen of its own accord.

If I *am* pregnant...

I'm not prepared for the whirl of soft emotions that follows that thought. Images flash through my brain of Christmases not spent all alone watching holiday movies, but with a little one discovering the magic of the holidays for the first time.

And Adam, his stern features softened with love as we both help our baby open their first Christmas present.

What the hell is wrong with you, woman?

I mentally slap myself to stop getting derailed by my clearly uterus-driven fantasies. There is absolutely *no* room for gushy emotions right now. Either it's anger at my boyfriend for locking me in his damn apartment, or it's panic at possibly being impregnated by said boyfriend. Those are the only two options I'm willing to accept, and until I pee on a stick, it's both. End of story.

AFTER EIGHTEEN MINUTES OF PACING, there's a knock. When I make it to the front door, there's a paper bag on the floor next to it. Inside I find three pregnancy tests, the saltines I asked for, as well as some nausea meds. I try not to feel too grateful to whoever was sent to pick up my supplies and rush off to the bathroom.

Five minutes later, I'm staring at the little plastic display on the first test.

The word "pregnant" is emblazoned across it.

NINETEEN
GILDED CAGE
HIM

There is only one number in my phone I've set to allow through during board meetings.

When it goes off in the middle of Roald's presentation of our record-breaking holiday sales, my heart spikes with adrenaline, and I answer immediately. "Eve? Is something wrong?"

"Come home right now!" she half-screeches into the phone. *"Right fucking now, Adam!"*

I'm out of my seat and rushing toward the door in two seconds flat. "I'm coming, baby girl. Tell me what's wrong? Are you hurt?"

"Mr. McCain—" Jim protests behind me. I ignore him —I ignore all of them, my heart slamming into my throat as horrific images of my beloved mate injured and bleeding fill my mind. I set off toward the elevator in a full sprint. "Eve! Tell me if you're hurt!"

"Just get home!" she all but snarls. Then she hangs up.

What the actual—?

I hit redial as I step into the executives elevator and smash the button for the ground floor. The doors close much too slowly, and a growl works its way out my throat as I wait for Eve to pick up. She doesn't.

I call Pete, the bodyguard I've stationed outside the front door to my penthouse, whose job it is to ensure Eve is safe while I'm not there. He answers on the first ring.

"Sir?"

"Is she hurt?" I snap into the phone.

A half-second's pause, then, *"No, sir. She's well."*

"Go check on her and make sure." Despite his reassurance, my heart's still pounding in my throat.

"Yes, sir." I hear a faint knock, then the sound of a door opening and closing. Footsteps, then a faint murmur of voices. One of them is distinctly female, and distinctly angry.

"She's not injured, sir," Pete says into the phone. *"Just upset."*

"Why is she upset?" I press, frowning as my pulse finally begins to slow.

Pete takes the phone away from his ear again, and I hear the murmur of his voice, but not what he says. I can't make out her response, either, but there's less screeching involved than before.

"She's saying you can ask her that yourself when you get here," Pete tells me after a moment. *"Would you like me to force her to answer now, sir?"*

I hear Eve's outraged squeak in the background, and snarl into the phone in warning. "Don't ever fucking joke about laying a finger on my woman again!"

"Sorry, sir. Is there anything more you need from me at this moment?"

I pinch the bridge of my nose, instincts still clamoring at me to murder one of my most trusted men for his ill-timed attempt at humor, and thoroughly frustrated that I have to communicate with my mate through another man. "No. Tell her I'll be there in twenty-five minutes. Then go back to your post."

"Yes, sir."

DESPITE THE CONFIRMATION that Eve is unharmed, the knowledge that she's angry with me gnaws at me, and sets my adrenaline on a hair-trigger. I haven't bonded her yet, playing the long game until she's ready to submit to my claim willingly, but that also means that she *technically* could leave me. Or she could at least try to. If I have to forcefully take her and make her mine, then we're both in for a lifetime of fucking misery.

I'd still choose it over losing her. I will, if she forces my hand. But the thought makes my gut feel leaden.

I love this woman in a way I didn't know I could love. I always knew meeting my mate would awaken possessive urges in me—it's one of the first things you're told as an alpha—but I didn't realize how completely she would rule my entire existence. Just the thought of her unhappy makes me want to dry heave. But if she left me?

I'd rather die.

I burst out of the elevator and barely acknowledge Pete as I stride to my front door in three steps and enter my home.

Eve's faint, but soothing scent fills my nostrils the moment I step inside, and I breathe in deeply, allowing it to settle my frayed nerves before I call out, "Eve, I'm here. What's the matter, baby girl?"

"Get in here!" she snaps from the living room area.

I head in. She's pacing in front of the coffee table, the scowl on her face softened by the look of panic in her eyes. I spot the pregnancy test on the glass surface behind her, and my heart gives a jolt of excitement.

Could it be...?

"You got me pregnant!" she accuses with a shaking finger pointed at the test, confirming my hope.

I can't contain the broad smile on my face at the news. "Oh, darling, really?"

"Why do you sound *happy?*" she stares at me,

eyebrows rising high with sheer surprise. "You understand this is crazy, right? We've known each other for two *weeks!* You even gave me a morning-after pill to prevent this! It's a disas—" Her panicked voice cuts off as realization strikes. Her pretty eyes narrow with suspicion. "You... did you... *plan* this?"

"Of course not," I lie smoothly. Still smiling, I step forward and pull her into my embrace, kissing her forehead and cheeks. "That would be insane. But I admit, every alpha instinct in me is ecstatic to know you're carrying my child. You'll be a wonderful mother, Eve. And I'll dote on you both every second of every day, I promise."

"Well, don't get too excited just yet," she growls, flashing me an annoyed glare even though she doesn't pull away from my affections. "I haven't decided if... if I'm keeping it."

Everything inside me stills. Surely, she wouldn't...?

I scan her face, my arms gentle around her waist despite the throbbing urge to clutch her tight and never, ever let her leave my side for so much as a second. She's scared, my sweet mate, afraid of how a baby will change her life, but behind the fear, there is a different kind of emotion: longing. A part of her wants this. It's my job to make her feel safe enough to embrace motherhood, and embrace *me.*

I look into her beautiful eyes with all the love I

contain. "Eve, it's your body. It's your choice. But please don't make it out of fear. I know we've been together for a short amount of time, but we're *fated*, baby girl. You and me—we're forever. Any children that come our way will be a wonderful solidification of our love, no matter when we are blessed with them."

I gently push a lock of hair behind her ear, caressing her cheek as her bottom lip quivers. "Please, my love. It may be soon, but you and me starting a family together... there is nothing I won't give to convince you that it's the right choice. Nothing I won't do."

She closes her eyes, inhaling deeply, and though we don't yet have a bond that ties us together, I can almost feel the tremble in her heart as she takes in my promise.

"Eve," I whisper. "Trust that I will protect every part of you. All I want is to make you happy, darling."

She looks up at me, and there's a thread of steel peeking through the vulnerability. "You say that, but you had me *trapped* in your apartment. Mr. Bodyguard out there refused to let me so much as go to the pharmacy—*on your orders*. That's not exactly something that makes me feel all warm and fuzzy about having your baby. In fact, it's something that would make any sane woman fucking *flee*."

I breathe slowly, evenly, tempering the roil of fury and panic in my gut as she mentions *fleeing* from me. There's no way on this green Earth I'll ever let that happen, but giving in to the alpha urges and telling her exactly who's in charge of her movements isn't going to make my mate willingly surrender her future to me.

Ordering Pete to keep her safely locked inside was a mistake; in a moment of weakness, I caved to my alpha instincts snapping and snarling to make sure my precious female is always exactly where I left her, safe and protected. And as I should have known, the second she realized she wasn't free to come and go as she pleased, the truth of my obsession became apparent. And that can't happen. Not until she's my mate and she's got my baby on her breast and there is no way out.

And even then, it would be better for both of us if she never finds out the extent of my possessiveness.

"I understand," I say softly, my face reflecting my regret and worry, if not the true cause. "I'm so sorry, Eve. I should never have done that. This... This is new to me too. All these *emotions,* these... primitive urges... I'm learning how to handle them in real time, and... I fucked up. Badly. All I wanted was to make sure you are safe at all times, but... yes. Restricting your freedom was... atrocious. Please, please don't let my primitive idiocy ruin our happiness. I swear to you, I will do better. So much better."

I will. I'll never be this obvious again. I gently stroke her cheek, my heart hammering in my chest. She's my everything. In a few short weeks, this small female now means more to me than my business, my family, my own life. There's nothing I wouldn't do to keep her content at my side.

"I just want to make you happy," I plead.

Caution is still evident in Eve's eyes as she looks up at me, but there's softness too—hope. She believes me. Thank all the stars in the sky, she believes me.

"You need to understand that I'm your equal," she says, voice stern, even if a small waver betrays the emotion she's struggling to contain. "I know you have... alpha stuff... going on, but you can't treat me like I'm your subordinate, or... like you own me. Got it?"

"Got it," I confirm, stroking my thumb down her cheek to her lips. "It won't happen again. I swear it."

"I mean it, Adam," she warns, pulling away from my caress to show me she's serious. "Despite what's happened between us, I'm not some weak-willed woman who can't stand on her own two feet. I'm *allowing* you to be all protective alpha—I don't need it to survive—and if I have to, I will be fine on my own. Baby or not."

"I know," I say, because it's what she needs to hear right now. "But you won't ever need to." Gently, I let my hand find her lower abdomen. "I'll treat both of you right —I promise, darling. And if I don't, yell at me, and I will instantly fix it. You're the love of my life—there's nothing I won't do for you, you understand?"

She swallows thickly at my words, her beautiful eyes turning shiny before she looks down, trying to hide the emotion in them. "The love of your life. I still... struggle to understand how that can be, after such a short amount of time."

"You're my Fated," I say softly, nudging her chin up, forcing her to look at me. "You know it's got nothing to do with length of time. I love you. When it all comes down to it, it's that simple. Whatever else you may feel about our courtship, I know you know my love is real. Look into my eyes, Eve. It's right there. Just for you."

Her eyes dart between mine, and I see the moment she gives up fighting against the inevitable. Tears spill over and drip down her cheeks, and when I draw her into my chest and wrap my arms around her, she sniffles.

"I love you," I say again, lips pressed against her scalp. "I'll always love you."

For a moment, her only response is quiet sniffling. Then, so quietly I almost miss it, she whispers, "I... I think I... love you too."

My heart slams hard against my ribs, and I let out a soft gasp into her hair. Every molecule in my body lights up from within as her hesitant confession fills my being like nothing I've ever experienced before.

She loves me.

I knew I wanted her to love me from the moment I accepted the truth of what she is to me. I wanted her willingly bound to my side.

I didn't anticipate how profoundly hearing those

whispered words would change my spirit, make it bloom until all I feel is deep, aching bliss.

She *loves* me.

"Eve," I croak, clutching her tighter to me. If I could absorb her into me, make her a part of my own flesh, I would. My skin itches with my need for her, for us to finally be one like we are supposed to. Breathing hard to keep control of myself, I pull back to look down at her, my fingers digging into her hips. "It's time, my love. I know you feel it too."

She stares up at me, gaze wide and lips parted. There is fear in her eyes, and if she tells me no, if she denies me, I don't know—

"Yes."

Yes.

Relief burns through my veins, euphoria in its wake so intense my vision blurs. *Yes.*

I lift her into my arms, feel the perfect weight on her against my body—another reminder of how we fit together in every way. How we were made for each other.

And now I finally get to claim her as mine.

TWENTY
LIKE A FUCKING CHRISTMAS TREE
HIM

The first time I had her, she was scared and tense, even as her body yearned for me as much as mine did for hers. This time, as I lay her down on my bed and crawl over her, my mouth hungry on her neck, jaw, collarbone, she's soft and pliant—eager for the pleasure I've trained her to expect.

"Your scent drives me wild," I moan into her ear before I bite the delicate lobe, my tongue playing with the pearl stud piercing it. "Everything about you makes me hard and so fucking needy."

She mewls in response and tilts her neck, baring her vulnerable throat.

The sweet submission has my blood pounding in my temples, and I groan deep in my throat and kiss my way down her breastbone. I don't have the patience to pull her sweater off, so I rip the soft yarn and yank the lacy bra underneath, exposing all her creamy, soft skin and those perfect tits topped with tight little nipples.

Eve makes some protesting sounds at my treatment of her clothes, but I'm too busy staring at her breasts to pay it any mind, imagining them full of milk. She'll be nursing my child soon enough. *Mine.*

"Oh!" Eve's startled exclamation ends on a breathy note as I latch onto one peachy pink nub and suck it deep into my mouth with a moan of longing. Every neuron fires in my brain, and *fuck yes,* this feels right. *Perfect.*

I'm barely aware of shredding her pants and underwear before my fingertips are met with wet, warm heat.

"Oh, shit, Adam!" she moans as I find the familiar little bulb of her clit and begin to stroke it with the pad of my thumb. Her hands find my hair and clutch me tighter to her breast, thighs spreading wider to give me better access.

I'm rougher with her than I've been since our first night, too desperate for what comes next to gently coax her body warm, but thankfully, my mate likes it with an edge of force. She soaks my hand in no time, my name spilling from her lips in rhythm with my thumb's tight circles on her pearl, and *fuck,* I *need* to be inside her.

Panting heavily, I pop my mouth off her nipple, the bud now flushed dark pink and extending an inch from the intensity of my suction.

She looks up at me, eyes hooded and curvy body bare in a pile of ripped fabric—looking like a picture-perfect sacrifice. Ready to be plundered.

My dick weeps at the sight, and as much as I want to worship every inch of her until she's begging to be fucked, I don't have the willpower to prolong this sweet torment. Not today. Not when I finally get to take what's mine.

"Are you wet for me, baby girl?" It's a rhetorical question—her slick juices coat her inner thighs and puddle under her ass, her body more than ready. I slip two fingers up in her warmth, reveling in her gasp of pleasure. She's not as tight as our first time—though I've not fucked her myself since then, I've made sure to gradually stretch her pussy with the toys I keep in my bedside cabinet, purchased specifically for this purpose. If I wasn't so fucking desperate, I'd give her an orgasm or two on a couple of the bigger ones before I split her on my cock, but she's just gonna have to grit her teeth and get through it. Judging from the roll of her hips and her happy little mewls as I finger-fuck her, it won't be too much of a hardship.

"You're such a horny little thing," I rasp, pumping my fingers into her sloppy pussy harder, faster. *Fuck,* the syrupy sounds of it go straight to my dick, making it impossible to think about anything other than how long it's been since her tight walls have been stretched around me. "You're gonna get your cunt fucked now, whether you like it or not."

Eve gasps out a breathy, *"Oh, god!"*, thighs opening wide as I pull my fingers from her and rip open my zipper with as much finesse as I spared on her clothes. I take a second to let my gaze sweep down her beautiful form—from her hooded green eyes and parted, panting lips, to her plump, suckled breasts, soft stomach, wide hips, and finally her swollen, pink pussy splayed and gushing for my cock.

I'm the luckiest man on the fucking planet that my girl likes it rough, because when I fall on top of her like a snarling beast and aim my cock straight at her small sex, her whimpered protests and mewls about me being *too big* are underscored by moans of pleasure. And right now, as her wet, tight heat finally kisses the crown of my cock, then reluctantly parts to swallow the meaty head, there's not a force on the planet strong enough to make me stop.

"Shit!" I groan as pure bliss fires into my pelvis and up my spine, short-circuiting my brain. *More.* The word pounds in my head, priming every cell in my body with singular need.

More, more, more!

I force my hips to Eve's, the movement slow despite my urgency. Her pussy grips my cock so, so tight, desperately attempting to halt my advance. But nothing's going to stop me from finally claiming what's mine, and the slippery proof of how much she craves it too betrays her reluctant flesh as I slide all the way in, forcing her to open wide.

"Shit, Adam!" she mewls, hands pawing desperately at my chest, pressing up against me in an attempt to alleviate the penetration, even as her body swallows me to the root.

I ignore her protests and press my face into the crook of her neck, breathing her into my lungs. *Everywhere.* I feel her everywhere... except the one place I need her the most. My heart aches with longing for our bond, the space for her already carved out of my flesh, just waiting to embrace her until I'll never be alone again.

"I love you," I gasp into her ear. "Tell me you love me too. Tell me you want me."

"I do," she whispers, voice strained from my presence in her sheath. "Adam, I do. But... but it hurts."

"I know, darling, I know." I pull back just enough to look down at her beautiful face. I drink in the pained pleasure etched across every feature, the longing for reassurance in her eyes as they search mine. "It'll all be worth it soon, I promise."

Slowly I pull my hips back, almost severing our intimate connection, before I plunge back deep, drawn by her pussy's siren song.

"Ah!" Eve's face contorts as she takes my cock, but there's thick pleasure in her cry.

God, she's perfect. She yields so beautifully, soft flesh accepting me all the way in, the edge of pain only enhancing her pleasure. *She wants me.*

Before her, before she lifted her hips and invited me in despite the ribbons I'd bound her with on our first night, I didn't realize how deeply I yearned to be wanted.

She is the only woman to ever crave me. Even if she hadn't been my Fated, I would have loved her.

"Oh, Eve." Her name tastes like a prayer on my tongue. "I'm gonna make you feel so, so good."

I do.

She screams at first, as my hips smack against hers and my cock pounds her little pussy into wide-spread submission. My skin smarts from her nails, but it only fuels my need to fuck her harder—show her who owns her cunt. Eventually, when she starts to plead for mercy and I take pity on her and thumb her stiff little clit, she breaks underneath me.

"Oh shit, Adam!" She clings to me, arms and legs clamping around my body as her pussy pulses frantically on my cock, sucking me deeper.

"That's it. Good girl. You're such a good girl," I moan into her ear, blind with the pleasure of her slick muscles trembling on my dick. The ache at the base of it makes me groan deeply, the urge to knot nearly insurmountable.

Not yet.

I withdraw halfway, easing the tightness against the

base of my shaft to stave off my knot. Eve's mewl of protest shoots lightning up my spine.

"I know, baby girl. You want me to plug you up and give you more sperm, even though I've already taken root in your womb." I nuzzle into her neck, inhaling the delicious scent of her. "It's the female imperative. Your cunt's always hungry for it, even if your conscious self dreads its potency."

"Ew, don't be such a fucking alpha," Eve groans underneath me swatting weakly at my side. "Sexism's not hot."

I grin into her neck and trace my tongue over her pulse point. "No? Then why's your pussy trembling at everything I say?"

"That's just exhaustion," she huffs, cringing away from my mouth to stop her body from continuing to commit mutiny. "I'm *not* into your weird little breeding kink. Knocking me up and then delighting in telling me my body wanted it is weird, Adam."

"Liar," I whisper into her ear as I slip my hand back down to her clit, massaging it gently. "I remember how hard you came when I bred your little pussy. And so do you. Your body wanted my baby even then."

"*Adam,*" she whines, squirming underneath me as I gently torment her hypersensitive little bud. "Stop..."

I flash her a grin and keep rubbing her, using the pad

of my thumb to push the protective hood back. "You know your safe word, baby girl."

She huffs underneath me, still twisting her hips back and forth in an unconvincing attempt at escaping my sweet torment. No mention of "mistletoe" falls from her sweet lips.

"That's what I thought." I pull all the way out, groaning softly at the way her slick walls cling to me, then snap back in with a wet sound when I finally draw free.

"God, you're beautiful when you're open like this." It takes all my willpower not to plunge straight back in. I cup her pussy, hiding her widened entrance with my hand to try and get my brain back under control, but the heat of her against my palm fries any remainders of reason.

Snarling with need, I flip her onto her stomach, yank her up on her knees by her ass, and then force my cock back up her pussy.

"Ah, shit!" Eve's cry rings through the bedroom, and she desperately clutches at the sheets as I plow all the way to her cervix.

Something snaps into place in the primitive lizard part of my brain.

Fucking Eve feels like nothing else in this world, but the second I enter her from behind, like an alpha's supposed to take his woman...

Every neuron in my brain lights up like a fucking

Christmas tree. I'm barely conscious of the *roar* that rips from my throat—all I sense is tight, aching pleasure and the animal need to *fuck*.

I take her so hard, her frantic screams turn to desperate wheezes for breath and the bed slams against the wall, denting the plaster and scoring deep grooves into the lacquered wooden floors. None of it matters. All that matters, all I can think about, is that once I'm done with her, no one's gonna question that this woman is *mine*.

I don't know how long I fuck her upturned pussy before the tension at the base of my shaft becomes unbearable. Instincts make me slam deep before grabbing her hips so she can't escape the inevitable.

Eve's hoarse wheezing turns to desperate wails as she claws at the bedding and fights to dislodge my rapidly swelling knot from her straining opening.

No fucking chance, darling.

I growl a warning as I yank her in harder against me. Her pelvic bones surrender, squeezing my knot tightly as it's forced in that last inch, until *finally*—

I roar as white-hot pleasure snaps through my entire being. My vision turns white as the coital tie locks us together and my balls release.

Pleasure is too small a word.

Eve. My Eve.

Mindlessly I fall on top of her, pushing her body deep into the mattress with my weight until she's immobile beneath me, panting and whimpering in climax—and bite down on her neck.

My airway fills with her rich pheromones, calling to me, begging for me. I break her skin, and her blood coats my tongue, rich and thick and coppery.

I feel our bond snap into place like a physical tightening deep in my heart.

Her consciousness floods through me, pleasure-drugged and blissful, filling me up until there is not a single empty space left in any part of my being. Everything I am, everything I'll ever be—she'll be right there with me.

Forever mine.

Christmas Eve - 1 year later

Snow falls like powder perfect little puffs of cotton, covering our balcony and Mattenburg beyond in a blanket of white.

From up here, the city looks almost serene—like a picture-perfect postcard—no sight of street grime or sounds of angry car horns disturbing my peaceful vigil. No matter how many times I come out here, I'll never get tired of this view.

My son makes a little squeaking sound, alerting me that he's waking up.

"Hello, baby," I coo, shifting my attention from the

city to his wool-clad little head barely poking up from the protective shelter of my winter coat. "Did you have a good nap?"

Jake squeaks again, drawing a gentle smile from me as I carefully hug him closer to my chest where he's been napping in his sling for the past two hours. Before he was born, I was frequently overwhelmed with anxiety that I wouldn't know how to be a mom, or that I'd regret having him. Adam always soothed my fears, promising me I'd make the best mother and that he would be there every step of the way, shielding and supporting me.

He kept his promise. Jake is three months old, and there hasn't been a day where Adam hasn't been fawning all over both of us, elbow-deep in his duties as a father and husband. I'm pretty sure no one at McCain Enterprises would believe their own eyes if they saw the fearsome CEO wrangling poopy diapers while cooing and coddling like a mother hen, but that's a sight I'm treated to on a daily basis.

I stroke a finger over my son's cheek and smile wider when he looks up at me with his dark, serious eyes. He looks so much like his father already, and barring while I was in labor, I haven't regretted him for so much as a second. I love this little man so much his dad occasionally gets jealous. Not that he ever tells me—but I feel the small stab in our bond when I've been entirely focused on the baby for too long.

Speaking of our bond...

I turn toward the glass door leading back into the penthouse. Adam is crossing the living room, his focus solely on me.

I light up in a smile, the warmth in my chest spreading outward at the sight of him.

Our bond flutters in response to my smile, a wave of affection reaching me from his end of it as he opens the door and joins me on the balcony.

"It's cold. You should be inside," he says, immediately wrapping an arm around me so he can pull both me and Jake into his chest. That's where he prefers to keep us both—safe and protected. If he could get away with it, I think he'd insist we both live in his protective embrace. Alphas are gonna alpha, as Noelle says.

"Well, hello to you too, Mr. Bossypants," I greet him with a teasing smile. "Welcome home. How was work?"

Adam's eyes soften at my greeting. "Welcome home?" he echoes in a murmur, nudging my chin up with the crook of his knuckle. "Oh, darling—you don't know how every part of me lights up when you say that. To know you're my home... you and the little one. I hate the days I have to leave you to go to the office, but getting to come home to you is the greatest gift of my life."

"You're wrong. I know exactly how you light up," I say softly. "I feel you in our bond. Your love is *my* greatest gift." I peer down at Jake. "Well, you and the munchkin."

Adam kisses the top of my head and touches the pad of his index finger to Jake's chin. Our son immediately latches onto it, then promptly begins to fuss at the size and lack of milk.

"He's hungry," Adam rumbles. "It's time to feed, Mama."

"He's not," I say with an eyeroll. "Trust me, when he's hungry, he wails like a siren and my breasts transform me into a dairy cow. He's just a spoiled little piglet who wants to comfort-nurse."

"Nevertheless, let's get you two back inside and out of this cold."

Without waiting for my compliance, Adam uses his arm around my shoulders to guide me back into the penthouse. Once inside, he helps me out of my winter coat and boots, then grabs Jake from the sling and cradle him in one arm so he can better herd me onto the sofa.

"I was thinking... since we're having people over tomorrow, we could watch your beloved Christmas movies tonight instead?" he asks as he pulls soft blankets and pillows down around me before handing me back the baby. "Just the three of us—celebrating our one-year anniversary."

"The one-year anniversary of what—Jake's conception, or his daddy's debut as a midnight burglar?" I tease.

Adam raises an eyebrow. "Careful with the sass, Mrs.

McCain, or *your* daddy will have to remind you what happens to bad girls, hmm?"

"All right, all right, I'll behave," I grin, cuddling deeper into the pile of blankets. "Thank you for remembering how much I love Christmas movies. I can't wait to see everyone tomorrow, but a night with my two favorite guys and some cozy holiday flicks sound like the perfect Christmas Eve to me."

Adam gives me a look as if to suggest he quite liked how we spent last year's too, and my abdomen tightens traitorously. However, before the smolder in my alpha's eyes can ignite, Jake decides it's time for dinner. An ear-splitting baby-yowl makes both of us cringe, all amorous intentions withering to dust.

Adam points at our son. "I told you he was hungry. You feed the beast, I'll make us some hot cocoa and light the fireplace."

"He wasn't hungry three seconds ago," I protest, but Adam's already headed for the kitchen, leaving me behind with our shrieking child.

"You really need to stop proving him right. He becomes absolutely insufferable," I mutter to Jake as I wrangle my already leaking breasts out of the nursing bra and offer him a nipple.

When Adam returns with two steaming mugs of hot cocoa topped with whipped cream and a sprinkle of cinnamon, I'm against the backrest, soft blankets pooled around my waist and with a content baby attached to my breast.

My alpha's eyes soften as he takes us in. "I'll never get tired of this," he murmurs. "My mate nursing my son. There's nothing more I want in life than moments like these."

"It's pretty magical," I agree, a loving smile playing on my lips as I look down at Jake. "Right up until he spits up all over me."

"You manage to make even baby sick-up look enchanting, my love." Adam bends to brush his lips against my scalp before he places the mugs of cocoa on the coffee table, then proceeds to light the fireplace. The crackle of burning wood fills the air, and soon the soft glow of candles joins the cozy ambiance as Adam lights several around the room, along with the fairy lights on the large Christmas tree, then switches off the overhead lighting.

"Got a preference on a movie?" he asks, grabbing the remote.

"Hmm... let's do *Christmas with the Kranks*. Something lighthearted and silly."

"As you wish, darling." Adam selects the movie, then climbs underneath the blankets with me and wraps his arms around my shoulder, gently tipping me in so I can rest against his chest. Jake, who's used to such maneuvers, doesn't so much as pause his nursing.

I snuggle closer to Adam, blissful all the way into my soul as we settle in. I really can't believe this is my life.

Some people might assume that the main perk of mating and marrying a billionaire is the fancy lifestyle and expensive gifts—and don't get me wrong, I'm spoiled as spoiled can be—but that's not the reason my life is perfect.

It's *him*. It's how completely he loves me, how completely he's given himself to me. Only a year ago, I was too tired, worn-out, and borderline depressed to even consider that I could have all the warmth and love and belonging I longed for. But since Adam's come into my life, it's been overflowing with all of it. I'm his now—I wear his mark on my neck, his bond in my heart, and his son on my chest. But he's mine too.

And I will never get enough of these quiet, private moments where my heart feels so full it's threatening to overflow.

Our cozy family moment lasts until I try to switch Jake to my other breast and get a flailing baby fist to my boob in retaliation.

"Ow! Come on, I hate when you leave me lopsided," I complain at my infant, who's decided that today, my right breast is the devil itself, and he's full anyway, *thank you very much, Mother.*

"I've got him," Adam says, amusement dancing in his eyes. He pauses the movie, scoops Jake out of my embrace, and takes my fussy hellspawn off to burp and be put down for a milk-induced coma.

I give my poor, bloated right breast a sad look before I climb off the couch to fetch my pump.

I've only just gotten the device attached when Adam returns *sans* baby.

"Went down without a fight today?" I ask.

"Like the angel he is," my mate confirms as he slips back under the blankets with me.

"*Angel?*" I snort. "Would an angel treat his own mother like one of her tits are poisoned? *I don't think so.*"

Adam grins at my theatrics, his eyes darting to the pump. "Is it uncomfortable?"

"Eh. It's better than being left full. But it makes me feel like a dairy cow," I grumble. "And *very* unappreciated, I might add."

"My poor darling. You're so very appreciated. And our son will come to be grateful for all that you do for him one day, I promise." He reaches out to cup my cheek. "But for now, why don't you let me help you ease the burden?"

I'm about to ask him what he means when he deftly reaches over to flick off the pump and detach the flange from my nipple. He flicks his eyes to mine, and in them I see dark, smoldering intensity. It's not desire—not exactly. It's something much deeper, something even more primal than lust, and it sends fire up my spine.

"Adam," I whisper.

"I was younger than Jake is now, just over a month old, when my brother and I were orphaned," he says softly. "When I tell you it touches something deep in me when I see you care for and nurture our son, I mean it goes into the very foundation of my soul. To see you so lovingly give him what I never had... I don't have the words to describe what it does to me. The wounds it heals."

"Oh, Adam. I'm so sorry. To lose your parents so young..." My heart aches for him. He's never mentioned his parents, and his brother only once or twice in passing, and I have wondered why. Now I know. From day one, my mate has gone to great lengths to show me his strength, his unwavering ability to be my rock, my foundation. This admission... Outside of the tears he shed when I brought Jake into the world, it's the first time he's truly shown me vulnerability.

"I won't pretend it didn't leave a mark on me beyond what I was ready to acknowledge, even to myself. But now, with you, with Jake... I've found what was taken from me." He gives me a tender look, then flicks his gaze to my breast.

I understand then what he needs.

I cup my breast and hold it out in silent invitation.

Adam makes a soft noise at the back of his throat and bends his head. He kisses my breast, then opens his mouth and captures my nipple—dark, swollen areola and all—between his lips.

"Ah." His first, gentle suckle makes my gasp echo through the living room as sensation shoots through every part of my body. I stare wide-eyed down at my mate, caught between the raw sexuality of his mouth on my breast and a deep, instinctive urge to nurture and protect brought to the forefront of my consciousness by motherhood.

There's a sensation then—a twinge, followed by a surge, like the breaking of a dam—and another soft noise escapes Adam's throat as my milk fills his mouth. Pure bliss. His eyelids flutter shut, and then he wraps his arm around my midriff and deepens his mouth's hungry contact with my breast.

I can't hold back a moan, and when a deep, rumbling purr sounds from my alpha in return, I clutch his head to me and surrender to the soul-deep knowledge that my powerful mate needs my love and protection as much as I need his.

CHRISTMAS DAY IS a blur of preparations for the afternoon's dinner party.

I'm desperately trying to get my wailing baby into a cute little elf costume so I can snap some pictures for the photo album when Noelle from Hall Events & Catering arrives with the food.

"I'll get the caterers set up, you get Jake dressed," I say, shoving the fussy baby into Adam's arms as I flee toward the kitchen. I'd die for my son in a heartbeat, but wrangling him into clothing when he's cranky and doesn't want to cooperate? Definitely better left to his daddy.

Noelle spots me as I enter the kitchen. She pauses mid-orders to one of her assistants and lights up in a surprised smile. "Eve, right? Eve... Compton? What a pleasant surprise."

"Well... Eve McCain now," I say, subconsciously rubbing my neck where my claiming mark is brandished.

"Ah. Congratulations." Noelle's eyes dart to my neck and darken a little. She looks like she'd rather extend her condolences, but she keeps a polite smile plastered in place. "I guess that answers the question of the identity of your suitor last Christmas. And explains the size of my tip."

I recall the story she shared with me about her friend who got forcibly mated, and her warning to me. Clearly Noelle isn't the biggest fan of alphas. Feeling a bit defensive, I say, "He's very generous, but that's not why I'm with him. We're Fated."

Noelle's smile tightens. "Oh, my apologies, Mrs. McCain. I didn't mean to imply anything like that. I'm very happy for you both. I hope you will think of Hall Events & Catering if you decide on a wedding."

I sigh softly. I can't blame her for her unease—before Adam, I also thought being mated to an alpha was some form of domestic slavery. On some level, it's kind of sweet of her to feel bad for a woman she's only met once, and for a grand total of twenty minutes.

I reach out, my responding smile warm and friendly, and give her shoulder a squeeze. "We wouldn't dream of hiring anyone else. I'll be in touch in the spring to discuss dates and menus. We're just waiting for the baby to get a few months older before we marry."

"Oh, you have a baby now? Congratulations! How old?" she asks.

"Three months," I say, my smile turning affectionate as I think about Jake. Then I see Noelle do the mental math, and sigh internally. "Yeah, he was an accident. But a very happy one."

I can see her trying her best to hold back the expression of sadness and concern for me that crosses her features, but she doesn't manage. "I'm... I'm sure."

She bites her lip, eyes darting to her two assistants who are busy unpacking pre-prepped food, and I know she's trying to stop herself from speaking out of turn and risking getting kicked out of what's undoubtedly one of their better-paid jobs of the year.

"Really, Noelle. I'm happy. I know what it looks like

from the outside—and you don't know how much I appreciate that you care; you don't exactly owe me anything—but I'm okay. More than okay." I give her shoulder another squeeze and pull back.

She smiles at me, looking like she's trying to believe me, but before either of us can say anything more, her eyes dart up over my shoulder just as I sense Adam entering the kitchen behind me.

"Eve, I need a moment," he rumbles. His face is schooled into a calm mask, like it usually is when we're in public, but I feel a slight twang of discomfort in our bond.

I smile lovingly at him—it's not unusual for my mate to be anxious when he's about to bring me into a public or semi-public setting—and ask Noelle to excuse me.

I follow Adam through the living room and into our bedroom, where Jake is happily sitting in his cute Santa's helper costume, looking like he never tried to kick me in the sternum in his efforts to avoid getting dressed.

"Oh, you got him in his outfit! Oh my God, isn't he just the sweetest little elf?!" I squee, immediately sidetracked by the adorableness that is my child.

I beeline to Jake, intent on pinching his round little cheeks, when Adam puts a hand on my shoulder. "Eve."

The seriousness in his voice diverts my attention, and I look up at my mate. "What's the matter, my love?" I ask, placing my hand on his chest where our mate bond hooks to calm him.

Adam folds his hand over mine on instinct, but there's still a twinge of discomfort in his eyes as he says, "My brother's coming to the dinner today."

I smile, surprised, but delighted. "Oh, really? That'll be nice, I..." My voice dies off at the intensity in Adam's gaze. "It... won't be nice?"

He takes a deep breath. "Alex is... the only family I have left, outside of you and Jake, but... we don't see each other often for a reason. I always invite him, but he usually ignores it. He just shot me a text, though, saying he'll come by to meet my mate and son."

"Maybe that's a good thing," I say, trying for optimism. "If he wants to meet us, and especially since he's choosing Christmas to do it, it might mean he wants a closer bond with you."

"Trust me, it's not a good thing," Adam rumbles, eyebrows bunching into a frown. "I don't want you or Jake alone with him, not even for a second. Do you understand?"

I blink. "Uh... that's kind of a scary thing to say, Adam. Why? If he's dangerous, I don't want him around Jake. Or my parents."

Adam shakes his head and reaches out to cup my cheek. "I'd never let him into my home if it put you in direct danger—you know that. It's just... He's..." He heaves a sigh, and I can feel his unease like a wave through our bond. "He's always been... complex. He's my brother. But... please, just promise me you'll stick by my side tonight."

I study my mate for a long moment, and not for the first time in our relationship, I get the distinct sense that he's not telling me everything I need to know. But his brother's not the only complex man in that family. I've known Adam had secrets and darkness from day one. I also know that as the days pass and our bond deepens, he will eventually tell me every dark secret and hidden pain, just like he did last night when he finally revealed why I hadn't seen or heard of his parents.

With a small sigh, I pat his chest and nod. "All right. I promise."

Adam draws me in to place a kiss on my forehead. His lips linger against my skin for a long second before he pulls back. "Thank you, mate."

I DON'T HAVE much time to wonder about Adam's cryptic warning about his brother. Our guests start arriving, and I'm soon swept up in a whirlwind of baby-cooing friends and relatives—as well as several strangers from Adam's side of the guest list. Not that I can blame them; Jake is, without a doubt, the most adorable baby in history —no, I'm not biased—and it would be impossible to resist his charms even without the cute elf costume.

"I still can't believe you banged McCain," Dana says

as we both watch my mom hogging the baby from his adoring fans. My friend takes a sip from her champagne flute and flashes me a wry grin. "Mostly because I imagine you would have been too terrified to unclench your vagina around him. I don't know how you didn't anxiety-barf when he asked you out."

I snort. "I'm not saying I didn't have some nerves the first time we met, but he's got a really sweet side in private." Also, he purred until my terror-clenching vagina buttered up like a biscuit, but I don't exactly tell people the truth about how Adam and I got together.

Dana gives me a dubious look. "Well, if you say so. Though I'm not complaining—I'm fully aware you doing the boss is the reason customer service got that pay increase, and easier targets."

"Just taking one for the team. Who wouldn't pick a mate just so her former colleagues can get a cushier ride? You're welcome." I give her a playful grin. In reality, I had very little to do with the wage boost or the more approachable performance targets. Turns out when Adam was busy stalking me last December, he listened in on several of my recorded calls and realized how shitty a job customer service is. I don't know how he didn't know that beforehand, but it was enough to make him want to boost morale in the department, even after he'd fired me.

"Your parents seem happy with your new beau. Or at least, your new beau's seed," Dana says, nodding at my mom, who's cooing at Jake. My dad stands over her shoulder, a gentle expression on his face that makes me feel soft inside as he allows his index finger to be used as a baby chew toy.

"Yup, they're thrilled. Kinda giving the impression they didn't expect me to ever settle down and have a family of my own." Not that I can blame them—at the height of my self-pity, I was wondering the same.

Dana wanders off to speak to her husband—possibly about starting Project Baby themselves, Jake just has that effect on ovaries—and I watch my parents dote on their grandchild. About 99.9% of me is thankful beyond words that I get to have this beautiful moment. 0.1% is hurt that it took me having a child for my parents to cancel their holiday-in-warm-weather plans and spend Christmas with me. Apparently I wasn't enough of a draw when it was just me, celebrating the holidays on my own.

"You're sad." The familiar rumble of my mate's voice sounds from behind me, hushed enough that no one else can hear.

I lean into his strong body, seeking the comfort of his touch on instinct. "No. Not really. Just... coming to terms with some things." I look up at him, and my stomach warms at the concern on his handsome face. I'll never be alone again; not for Christmas, nor any other day of the year. For the rest of my life, Adam will be there, loving and supporting me every step of the way. As I will for him.

I reach out and twine my fingers with his. "I love you. I'll always love you. You know that, right?"

My alpha's face softens, and the gentlest smile I've ever seen touches his lips. "My Eve. I will never stop thanking Fate for you," he whispers, tenderness dancing in his dark eyes as he raises my hand to his lips and kisses my knuckles.

We stare into each other's eyes for a long, sweet moment, the unspoken vows of affection passing through our bond and deep into my heart.

It lasts until the front door opens, and Adam turns his attention from me to the newcomer. His large body tenses almost imperceptibly.

I follow his gaze to the door. A large, dark-haired alpha stands there, and a wave of surprised recognition sweeps through me. He isn't the spitting image of Adam, but his high cheekbones, strong nose, and the cut of his jaw is almost identical.

"Your brother, I take it?" I murmur to my mate.

"Mmhm," he grunts, giving my fingers a squeeze before releasing them. "I'd best go say hello."

His posture is relaxed as he approaches the other alpha, but I feel the tension he's hiding simmering in our bond. He really wasn't exaggerating when he hinted at their relationship being anything but uncomplicated.

But, complex or not, this is my brother-in-law, and he's made the effort to come see me and Jake.

I scoop up my son from my reluctant mother, then make my way over to the newcomer, a friendly smile plastered on my face.

"Hi, you must be Alex. It's so nice to meet you. I'm Eve, Adam's mate, and this is... Jake." It's all I can do to not choke on my baby's name, because just then, Alex turns to look at me, and something cold and awful grips my spine.

"Eve," he repeats slowly, his voice dark velvet over icy steel. His dark eyes travel down my body, curiosity rather than lechery in their depths. Then they flick back up to my face, and I take an automatic half-step backward.

I've never met someone like Alex in my life. He *looks* perfectly normal—handsome like his brother, even—but there is something... deeply, horribly *wrong* with him. Every hair on my body stands on end as his gaze bores into mine, almost as if the instinct charged with my survival recognizes a danger I can't see with my naked eye. But oh, boy, do I *feel* it. It's like this man in front of me is the living embodiment of foreboding.

Alex mercifully turns his disturbing eyes from me to his brother. "She's... very vulnerable, isn't she? Soft. You must wake up terrified every day, especially with a baby on her breast. If cornered, a mother will almost always choose her child's life over her own. It's instinctive."

"*No one* is cornering Eve," Adam growls, his voice low enough that none of our other guests can hear, but the warning is unmistakable. "Your text said you wanted to meet my mate and son. If you're not in the right head-space to do so, you can leave."

Alex smiles faintly, his chilling focus returning to me. "No need to get defensive, brother. They're kin, after all. We protect our own. Don't we?"

So swiftly I don't manage to move away, he grabs the hand I'm not holding Jake with and raises it to his lips, placing a kiss on the back of it that sends chills down my spine.

"Welcome to the family, my dove," he says.

"Um. Thank you," I manage stiffly.

"*Alex*," Adam growls.

Alex sighs softly and releases my hand. His gaze lands on Jake. He stares silently at him for a long moment before he reaches out and gently strokes his cheek. It takes everything I have not to yank my baby out of his reach.

"Such a fragile little thing he is," Alex murmurs, as if he's a million miles away. "Take good care of my nephew, sweet dove." Without another word, he walks off, mingling with our other guests.

"What. The hell. Is wrong with him?" I hiss through clenched teeth as I stare wide-eyed after the disturbing alpha.

Adam sighs softly and wraps his arm around me,

pulling me into the comfort of his embrace. "Our upbringing was... difficult. He... came out of it with more scars than me."

I wait for him to elaborate, but he doesn't.

"Adam... is he... safe? To have in our home?" I whisper, anxiously following my brother-in-law with my gaze as he effortlessly mingles with our guests, a charming smile spreading on his handsome face. From the smiles of the people he interacts with, they don't get the same instant sensation of *wrongness* from him as I did, almost as if he allowed me to see past the mask he usually wears around others.

"Yes," my mate says softly. "And even if he wasn't, know that I wouldn't hesitate to put a knife in his heart to protect you or Jake. But the fact that he sees you as kin makes this... easier. He lives by his own moral compass, but family is sacred to him. As it is to me." He turns to look at me, gentle resignation in his eyes. "He won't hurt you, Eve, but sometimes his idea of protection isn't much better. Just... stay by my side tonight."

I swallow thickly, but nod. I've got zero problem with sticking to Adam like glue if it means his creepy brother keeps his distance.

I DO my best to ignore Alex's presence, and by the time the caterers begin to bring out the food, I've mostly succeeded. The guests' oohs and ahhs fill the room as Noelle places the enormous turkey on the center of the table, and I shoot her a grateful smile.

"It looks beautiful," I tell her. "And it smells delicious."

She grins. "I should hope so—I've been babying this bird for the past fourteen hours. We'll bring out the rest of the sides now. Just give me a shout when you're ready for dessert."

"Will do. Thanks," I say, turning my focus back to my guests, my heart swelling with gratitude at the gorgeous food and the company here to celebrate with us.

Everyone's looking at the food, happily chatting to one another about how lovely it looks. Everyone but Alex. When my eyes catch on him halfway down the table, he's not looking at the turkey.

He's looking at Noelle.

My heart drops at the intensity in his eyes, and the look of hunger on his face that has nothing to do with the food she's placed in front of him. I recognize that expression all too well; it's the same way Adam looked at me the night he broke into my home.

If Noelle's still as unenthusiastic about alpha lovers as she seemed last year, I think she's got some uncomfortable times ahead.

WANT MORE FROM ADAM?

EVEN AFTER I finished writing *Holiday Intrusion*, Adam refused to leave my head. He wouldn't stop popping into my brain all, *"You know what I did after meeting Eve? You want to find out how I planned to make her mine, don't you?"*

And the bastard was right. So... I wrote a bonus scene from his point of view starting immediately after Eve fled the mistletoe-elevator incident back in chapter 2.

If you want a little more time with our favorite stalker CEO, you can find the extra bonus scene at www.nora-ash.com/extra

Love,
Nora

Meet the Alpha who'll chase you down, kill your enemies and claim you in the middle of their bloody remains...

ALPHA

A shadow moves in the darkness, and death follows in its wake. The faint light from the city reaching into the park gleams off cold steel as the newcomer finally makes himself known.

He whirls across the grass, and I hear the sick sound of metal slicing through flesh followed by wet gurgling. When the two remaining men fall to the ground, he finally stands still, staring down at the unmoving bodies. His victims.

He is a huge man, bulging muscles clear even in his shadowed outline. An alpha, no question about it.

It's not until he turns his attention to me that I notice the black mask covering the top half of his head.

No one with good intentions ever hides their face, and a new layer of goosebumps break out across my skin as I stare up at the silent alpha.

The silent killer.

Will he hurt me, too?

I don't dare take my eyes off the dark figure to glance at the slumped bodies I know litter the ground around us, but every hyper alert part of me knows they're there, the deadening silence enveloping us an imposing contrast to the fight just seconds ago.

He tilts his head, obviously looking at my still-sprawled form on the muddy ground, and my heart threatens to jump out of my throat.

"P-please. Don't kill me." It's a ridiculous plea, but I can't stop it from spilling past my lips even if someone who can kill with such ease as this alpha is unlikely to have an ounce of mercy in his body.

The alpha grunts, a sound of disgust or surprise I'm not sure, but when the steel dagger in his hand gleams against the faint city lights, it's because he wipes it on his pants before shoving it into its sheathe. A large hand extends toward me, hovering in the air above my face.

I stare mutely at the appendage. Is he... offering me a hand up?

The gesture seems so grotesquely out of place, considering the gore surrounding us, that I can't help the snort of amusement that breaks out of my fear-clenched throat. Horrified with myself, I slap a hand across my mouth, but he doesn't react to my faux pas. The hand still hovers above me, waiting for me to grasp it.

Well, if he wanted to kill me, he would have done so by now. Probably.

I move my hand from my mouth and carefully place it in his, my fingertips brushing over soft leather as I do. He's wearing gloves.

Strong fingers close around my hand, and without preamble I am hoisted up off the ground to stand on my own, shaky feet. The alpha releases his hold on my hand the second I've regained my balance.

"T-thank you," I manage, not entirely sure if I mean for the hand up, or for saving me from the gang.

He saved me.

It's not until that moment it fully dawned on me that... that he killed those men to... save me?

"Did you... you killed them... for me?" I babble, my panic reaching new and unprecedented heights. "Oh God, am I an accomplice to murder? Shit, *fuck,* this day just cannot get any worse!"

It's not the sanest response to getting rescued from gang rape, some far-away part of me recognizes, but that part is somehow removed from the rest of me—who's busy having a complete break down. Pants around my ankles, top ripped and smeared in mud and the tone of hysteria clear in my increasingly high-pitched voice.

A large hand closes around my right shoulder, the strength in it evident from even the light squeeze that finally breaks through my hysteria.

"Calm yourself."

His voice is deep and gruff and one hundred percent *alpha.* It resonates down my spine and into my muscles, easing some of the tension in my body as only the authoritative command of an alpha can. I stare up mutely up at him, not sure if I am thankful that he's stopped my spiraling breakdown or angry that a murderous stranger can have that sort of impact on my body. I shouldn't be any kind of *calm* right now, but my treacherous biology gives exactly zero fucks about what I think it *should* be doing.

"I'm sorry," I say when he releases his grip on me again, finally realizing that freaking out on the guy who just saved me from the ultimate pain and humiliation is neither polite nor particularly smart. Even if he did just kill five men in cold blood in front of me, and I still have no idea what he wants from me. If it's sex he's after, he could have taken it by now, and my life along with it.

I blame his alpha-influence over my nervous system for why I'm not more scared of him. Sure, my pulse is still drumming rapidly in my throat, but I'm not frightened for my life. I should be. I should be begging him for mercy or trying to run from him, however futile such an act would be.

"Um... I really appreciate it." I feel stupid even as I say it, partly because of the sentiment and partly because it finally dawns on me that my pants are still around my ankles. I want to bend to pick them up, but the urge to not take my eyes off him is stronger. Yeah, I might not be as scared as I ought to be, but even his influence can't completely numb out the rational voice in my brain screeching that I'm alone in an abandoned park with a masked killer. He's a predator, there's no question about it, and every instinct in my body's telling me that sudden movement is a very bad idea.

"I don't have any money on me, but—" My lips quiver when he takes a single step toward me.

"B-but if I can do anything to repay you, I will," I quickly stutter, the threat of his presence suddenly much sharper in the most primal part of my brain thanks to the too-close proximity of his huge body.

Yeah, he's an alpha all right. It's not just the sheer size of him—it's the powerful aura rolling off him in waves even as he keeps his body immobile in front of me. That unquestioning demand for submission. The completely unprovoked thought that he probably smells headier than any other male on the planet flashes through my mind, and I blink in shock at its unexpected passing.

"You think I am some vigilante saving damsels in distress in the hopes of a reward?"

His voice is surprisingly soft, though the alpha gruffness in it never wavers. It is velvet wrapped over an iron core, and it makes me shake, though I don't know why.

"No." There is nothing velvety about my own voice. It's as shaky as my body, hoarse from stress and screaming. It's the voice of prey, and I hope it doesn't trigger whatever violent instincts an alpha his size is bound to have in abundance. "I don't. But... who are you? I-if you don't mind me asking." I tag the last bit on when the idiocy of asking a masked killer for his identity hits me like a brick wall.

"I know who *you* are," he says, ignoring my question. I feel his eyes still shaded in the darkness trail up my body. The sensation makes me shiver despite the blood in my veins heating up. *Fucking alpha.* I never feel anything but mild fear and loathing for his kind—why is he different?

"You're the reporter who nearly caused a riot at Town Hall last night."

I gape up at him. "H-how do you know that?" Real smart admitting to that, but the surprise of his statement catches me off guard.

He cocks his head, the shape of his sensual mouth flattening into a line. "Who do you work for?"

"K-KTP News," I stutter, taken aback by the suddenly threatening undercurrent to his otherwise calming voice.

"I know your network," he sneers, and this time I'm sure I can detect anger. My ever-looming fear hikes up several notches in response. "What I don't know is who sent you to that press conference high as a kite on heat-hormones. Who's behind this? Who wants to discredit the Liberals bad enough to shove a foolish young girl on the cusp of Presenting into a roomful of alphas?"

Despite the insult of being called '*a foolish young girl*' at the age of twenty-six, I can't muster so much as a frown. For every word his voice gets sharper, and the alpha pheromones in the air turn from placating to aggressive. He's *pissed*, and it's wreaking havoc on my already frayed nerves.

"I.... I wasn't on any hormones. I-it just happened. I'm not trying to discredit anyone, I swear!"

"Bullshit," he hisses, and then he's right in front of me, the heat from his body radiating against mine. He grabs me by the back of my neck, cupping my head as he pulls me in while simultaneously dipping his face to my throat.

I whimper in confused panic, but the firm grip on my neck keeps me from trying to fight him off. I stand frozen, paralyzed like a kitten in its mother's grasp, and stare with huge eyes as he draws in a deep breath of my scent. His breath tickles across the skin of my throat, making every hair on my body stand on end, my nipples harden painfully against my ruined top.

"You still smell like desperation and sex." This time his voice is a low growl, the frustration still evident, but there's also a rich, sultry quality to it. "Like *heat*. Tempting any alpha you pass by. Do you *want* to get raped?"

There's something in his voice, that heated, sultry note, that suddenly makes it clear what his intended payment for my salvation might be. But instead of the outrage I *should* feel, something tense low in my abdomen melts in response. It's not until I realize I've gone lax in his grasp, letting him support my weight with his that it dawns on me what I'm doing. What I'm offering.

"No!" I jolt backward and away from him, the sheer shock at my own reaction to this stranger, this *killer*, jolting me out of whatever spell his presence is weaving over my confused mind. "Absolutely not!"

He lets me stumble out of his grip and a few steps away, and I nearly trip over my own pants.

Shaking like a leaf from how close I was to letting this stranger do what he wants with me, I bend to pick up my pants. I no longer care if I have to take my eyes off him to do so, I need to not be so exposed anymore.

My fingers are stiff from cold and shock, and the button and zipper are bust. Awkwardly, I cling on to them with one hand as I look back up at the alpha. I open my mouth to tell him thank you again for saving me, but I'm leaving now—but just then, our eyes finally meet and all that escapes my parted lips is a low grunt.

His eyes are a cool shade of gray—the eyes of a ruthless alpha for sure. But behind the facade there's something else. Something wild and deep and primal, and it's pulling on a part of me I never knew existed until this very moment.

Out of nowhere, a sharp twinge in my abdomen makes me whimper from surprise and pain, and I keel over, losing my grip on my pants as I rest my hands on my bare knees for the few seconds it takes before my body is released from the unexpected spasm. It is gone as swiftly as it came.

I blink, slowly straightening up.

No. No, no, no, not again! I stare at him, wide-eyed, the accusation of using some sort of biological warfare against me not completely formed in my mind when I'm hit by the next wave. This time, it's... different, and I recognize the heat blooming out from deep inside of me before arousal shakes through my body in fitful waves.

It can't be. Please, no.

The groan I involuntarily send into the air between us sounds like a pleading, *"Ooh"*.

Oh God, it's really happening again.

Slick moisture rushes from my core, flooding my pussy until a river of fluids gushes out and soaks my broken pants as my body presents for him, the alpha it mistakenly believes has been posturing for my favor.

Despite my body's mutiny, I feel my sense of civilization take a firm hold as the deepest blush of my lifetime spreads over my entire body. I slap the hand not clinging to my pants in front of my face with a humiliated whimper, curling in on myself while the pleasurable shocks preparing me for him—this killer—rake through me, stronger than anything I've felt before.

"Oh God!"

I whine through the expulsion of liquids and the opening of my channel in anticipation of his claiming, too mortified to look at the man who's done nothing to incite this response from my body.

It must be the adrenaline, the conquering of other alphas to save me, it must be ... My thoughts are struggling to find reason during the onslaught of my most basic instincts, but finally I am released from the tremors, my body having completed the preparation. From my disastrous experience last night, I know my sex is flushed and opened, slick and ready for penetration, but all I sense is the soaked state of my thighs and clothes and the utter and complete humiliation of this horrific situation. Maybe, when I think back to this night later on, the worst parts will be the near-rape or the witnessing of a mass murder, but right now, those things are astonishingly hard to even remember.

He must think I am a lunatic. And he'd probably be right. I straighten slowly, forcing my hand from my face so I can apologize. I don't care who he is—there is no excuse for this vulgar display. None.

"I... I'm really sorry, I don't know why this keeps happening to me." My voice is a humiliated whisper.

He cocks his head at me, and I have to fight myself to not hide my face behind my hand again.

"I'm really sorry," I repeat, a frantic note making my voice shrill again. "This should never happen—it's so wrong, I'm so sorry." My fingers clutch at the fabric around my midriff, and I fumble desperately to secure them to preserve at least an echo of my dignity. I don't manage to make any headway before the air pressure shifts and I automatically glance up.

Once more, the alpha is right next to me, close enough to notice that his eyes now appear fully black, swallowed by dilated pupils. Without my conscious command my fingers release my pants, letting them slide back down.

Oh, God.

His nostrils flare, and a new rush of wetness drizzles down my thighs, as if my body's responding to his obvious scenting of me. Like I wasn't already drenched enough for even a normal person to smell my pheromones—they're so thick in the air I can practically taste them.

A wry smirk pulls on his full lips, and in that single change of expression the ever-present predator leaps to the forefront.

"Oh, God!" I gasp as I see him removing the leather glove from one hand, carelessly letting it fall to the ground. My body clenches and shudders in primal recognition of what is written all over his face, even if my conscious mind still refuses to acknowledge it.

When his thick, warm finger reaches between my legs and dips into my slit I wish I'd saved the outburst for this. He pulls it up, dragging it through my folds all the way from my sopping hole to the aching nub burning at the top before lifting the digit slowly, provokingly, to his lips. I stare at him in shock when he opens his mouth to suck my fluids off.

His eyes flutter shut, a deep growl resonating from his throat and all the way into my spine sending a new gush down my thighs, and I whimper pathetically. Half from need, half from fear, because even before he says it I know there's only one way this can go now.

Black, primal demand flashes against me when his eyes open once more, the smirk still present—taunting.

He knows I won't be running this time.

ALPHA TIES

Alpha

Feral

Intrusion

PROTECTOR

Rage

Treachery

Bound

THE OMEGA PROPHECY

Ragnarök Rising

Weaving Fate

Betraying Destiny

DEMON'S MARK

Branded

Demon's Mark

Prince of Demons*

ANCIENT BLOOD